Dayanita moaned, lifting her hands to hold his arms that were crossed over her body, tilting her head to give him better access, thrilled to feel the rasp of his tongue against her fast-beating pulse.

Harshvardhan pressed soft kisses from her neck down the slope of her shoulder, his teeth joining his tongue as he took small nips of her silky skin, careful not to mark the golden smoothness.

Her head fell back on his shoulder as Dayanita gave herself up to his caresses, her small teeth biting into her lower lip, feeling as if her whole body was on fire.

Harshvardhan turned her around in his arms, his hands at her back now, drawing her close to his aroused body, his lips on her hot cheek as he traced a path towards the corner of her mouth.

"Nita?"

"Kiss me, Harsh. Now."

ABOUT THE AUTHOR

Sundari Venkatraman is an Indie Author who has 62 books to her credit. These books have consistently featured in the Top 100 Bestseller Lists on Amazon Kindle, in both romance as well as Asian Drama categories. Her latest hot romances have all been on #1 Bestseller slot in Amazon India for over a month.

THE WOOING OF THE SHREW is the third book in The Thakore Royals trilogy; and based on Indian Contemporary Royals. This kindle book remained in #1 Bestseller position on Amazon India for two whole months from its release.

Even as a child, Sundari absolutely loved the 'lived happily ever after' syndrome and she grew up on a steady diet of fairy tales, Phantom comics and Mandrake comics. It was always about good triumphing over evil and a happy ending after the protagonists surmounted all unexpected obstacles.

Once she entered her teens, Sundari switched her loyalties from fairy tales to Mills & Boon. While she loved reading both of these, she kept visualising what would have happened if there were similar situations happening in India; to local heroes and heroines. And of course, the joy of vanquishing the ubiquitous evil villains! Her imagination soared and she happily ensconced herself in a rosy romantic cocoon for many years.

Then came the writing—a true bolt from the blue! And Sundari Venkatraman has never looked back.

LIST OF BOOKS
BY
SUNDARI VENKATRAMAN

Books by Sundari Venkatraman

Standalone novels
The Malhotra Bride
Meghna
The Madras Affair
An Autograph for Anjali
Twin Torment
Finding Anya
Mr. Perfect
Man Friday
Her Prince Charming
Love in Agartha
Arjun's Penance
The Floundering Author
Once Bitten Twice Lucky
Ryan Finds a Bride
Tinder Loving Care
Shaan Gets Hitched
For Better or For Worse
Heartthrob
Call of the Heart
Sing For Me

Collection of shorts
Matches Made in Heaven
Tales of Sunshine

The Groom Series Trilogy
#1 Groomnapped
#2 Gobsmacked
#3 Grounded

Dashavatar (Indian Mythology)
MATSYA: The First Avatar
KURMA: The Second Avatar
VARAHA: The Third Avatar
NARASIMHA: The Fourth Avatar
VAMANA: The Fifth Avatar
PARASHURAMA: The Sixth Avatar

The Writer's Toolkit (Non-fiction)
Publishing Your Book on Amazon
KDP

Marriages Made in India Series
#1 The Runaway Bridegroom
#2 Her Smitten Husband
#3 His Drunken Wife
#4 Her Secret Husband
#5 The Casanova's Wife
#6 Her Bohemian Husband

The Bansal Legacy Trilogy
#1 Simha International
#2 Rose Garden International
#3 Maharaja International

Written in the Stars Series
#1 Scorpio Superstar
#2 Leo's Desire
#3 Taurus Temptation
#4 Virgo's Krush

The Thakore Royals Trilogy
#1 The Marriage Predicament
#2 Tied in Knots
#3 The Wooing of the Shrew

Romantic Shorts
#1 Chahti Hoon Tumhe
#2 Beauty is but Skin Deep
#3 Madeinheaven.com
#4 An Arranged Match
#5 The Reluctant Bride
#6 Shweta ka Swayamvar
#7 Papa's Girl
#8 Red Rose Dating Agency
#9 Rahat Mili
#10 Reema's Matchmakers
#11 The Matchmaker's Dream

The Princess Series
(Historical Romance)
#1 The Passionate Princess
#2 The Rebel Princess

T H E
Wooing of the
S H R E W

THE THAKORE ROYALS
BOOK 3

SUNDARI VENKATRAMAN

FLAMING SUN

ISBN 979-8-89002-858-7

Edited by: Preeti Arora
Beta Read by: Rubina Ramesh
Cover Illustration: Unaiza Merchant
Launched by: The Book Club

DEDICATION

#metoo & #nameandshame are tags that are powerful and extremely useful in the right hands. But what if they are misused? This book is for those who have been adversely affected!

AUTHOR'S NOTE

There are a number of modern royals in India. But for the sake of my story, the royals and their territories that I have used, are all part of my imagination. While the places Udaipur and Baroda exist, the kingdoms, palaces and the characters don't exist outside my imagination.

"How dare you? How dare you undress me with your gaze?" Sparks of fury flew from Dayanita's chocolate brown eyes, impaling the man who was standing a few feet away from where she had been dancing until a minute ago, checking her out.

"Huh!" Harshvardhan's lips curled to the left even as his right eyebrow rose up to touch the lock of hair falling over his wide forehead. "I don't get you." His eyes continued to rove over her gorgeous features, unable to resist. She was too beautiful for words, her sharp nose stopping short of being classy with the tip tilting that little bit. Her eyes were large with the longest lashes he had ever seen, making him wonder if they were for real. Her oval face with silky cheeks ended in a pointed and determined chin that challenged him along with her words.

"I've been noticing you since long. You have been checking me out for the past fifteen minutes. How dare you strip me with your gaze? Do you know who I am?" Dayanita was beyond furious. He had some guts, pretending not to understand what she meant. If he thought she was one of those females who cowered in front of alpha males, he had another think coming his way. She would kick his ass to hell and back.

Harshvardhan choked as he tried to control his laughter. "Are you saying that *you* were checking *me* out?" he asked on a gasp as his mirth refused to be curbed, laying stress on the words 'you' and 'me'. "That too for more than fifteen minutes? Get a life, will you! And by the way, I don't know who you are. Would you care to enlighten me?"

"Hey!" Dayanita walked forward to stand toe-to-toe with him, her eyes on a level with his chin. She didn't care for the fact that she had to tilt her head to meet his eyes. Lifting a hand, she hit him on his chest with the flat of her palm, wincing as it felt as if she had slapped a rock. "Just because you are a man, don't think you can get away with anything. I…"

"Hello! Wait a minute there, before you say things that you might regret. Aren't you quite the motormouth!" He straightened up from his lazy stance from where he had been leaning against the bar, his legs crossed at the ankles, while he sipped from his glass of whiskey and soda. Keeping the glass carefully on the bar, he turned back to look into her eyes from his supreme height of six feet three inches. Not that she was all that shorter than him at five feet, nine inches plus the four-inch stilettos that graced her dainty feet. But it still felt good to be that little bit taller. He leaned closer to her face and said, "Now tell me, what's bothering you?"

"Your gaze," she insisted, pointing her index finger between his eyebrows, a trifle too close for comfort, as she continued to glare into his smoky grey eyes. "How dare you continue to stare at me?"

Her finger nail made him squint, as he wondered if she might poke into one of his eyes, maybe even both. But he refused to back down as he stared deeply into her brown gaze, finding himself melting. It was difficult not to smile as he asked in a casual tone, "Tell me something. How would you know that I was staring? Unless you have been looking at me too?" He tilted his head to one side, wiggling his eyebrows at her, a grin slowly emerging on his face as he saw signs of an explosion right in front of his face.

And explode she did! Stamping her foot in fury, Dayanita slashed a hand through the air, too close to him for comfort, snarling, "Men!" She shook her head, her silky hair whirling around her, obviously at a loss for words, but refusing to be beaten by his logic. He had been staring at her and she wanted to tell him off for it. That his gaze travelling over her body made her all tingly and aware, only fuelled her temper all the more.

"Yes? You were going to say?" He egged her on, an amused glint in his eyes. "I'm dying to know your esteemed opinion on "men"." He lifted his hands and drew quotation marks in the air. "And I'm sure you will allow me to tell you what I think of "women"." He was openly laughing by now.

It was a wonder that the two of them could hear each other talk at Exchange LA, a popular and noisy night club in Los Angeles. The place was packed with dancers jostling against each other as they swung to the fast numbers churned out by the disk jockey. Prince Harshvardhan Singh Gaekwad from Baroda, also a popular Bollywood film-star, had arrived in Los

Angeles only that morning and at the disco, barely half an hour ago. Not finding a place to sit, nor having a partner to dance with, he had been leaning against the bar with his drink when his eyes fell on the slim, but lissom beauty in a shorter than short, figure hugging dress of gold lamé that barely covered the top of her sexy thighs, while faithfully following the shape of her pert bottom. She was definitely drool worthy. And yes, she had met his gaze with her own every time she turned in his direction. That had only thrilled him and he had been biding his time before walking across and joining her on the dance floor. Only she beat him to it when she sought him out to tell him off.

Yes, the truth was that he had been checking her out. As for undressing her with his gaze, that was one thing he wasn't going to admit even to himself. Harshvardhan couldn't allow any woman so much power over his thoughts, especially on their first meeting.

"Shit!" Dayanita stamped her foot again before taking an about turn to walk in the opposite direction.

"Hey!" he called out, "wait. You still haven't really told me who you are. You aren't going to leave me here without that knowledge to make my knees tremble, are you now?"

She half-turned her head, showing the middle finger of her right hand as she continued to walk towards the opposite end of the room.

Harshvardhan burst out laughing, unable to stop himself. She was definitely something and he couldn't wait to find out who she was.

It took him but a few minutes to find out enough details as she had come along with a group of students from the Los Angeles Film Academy where she was doing a course in screenplay writing.

A furious Dayanita went to sit at a table for six on the farthest side of the club, where Jake was sitting all by himself. The two of them had come along with four other friends. They had been dancing when Dayanita had noticed someone staring at her and gone over to pick a fight with the man. She had simply left Jake by himself on the dance floor, walking away to tackle the stranger.

Jake didn't even consider following her since he knew that the independent Dayanita preferred to handle things by herself and wouldn't thank him for his efforts if he had tried to give her his support during the altercation.

"Hey, are you okay?" Jake placed a hand on her shoulder now, bending down to catch her eye. He was a blue-eyed American who made his attraction to Dayanita very obvious. Not that it had got him anywhere with the Indian princess.

"Yep, I'm good." Dayanita gave him a nod, shimmying her shoulder in such a way that his hand fell off it. She didn't like being touched. She lifted her glass of vodka and orange and took a deep swig from it, grimacing at the taste as the ice had all melted and the cocktail was diluted.

"Let me get you another," said Jake, immediately getting up from his chair.

"Not the same, Jake. I'd rather have a beer."

Jake took off to get her what she wanted.

"Who was that?" asked Andrea, flopping into the chair next to Dayanita with a wide smile on her face. While the beautiful looking brunette from Greece had been dancing a fast number with Dino from Italy, she couldn't help but notice the heated argument between Dayanita and the delicious hunk who had been standing at the bar.

"I don't know, nor do I care." Dayanita replied to her friend before swigging directly from the beer bottle that Jake handed her.

Andrea's smile turned into a grin. "Oh really! For strangers, it looked like the two of you had a lot to say to each other."

Dayanita laughed out loud, her anger disappearing. She wrinkled her nose at Andrea, saying, "Seriously! I know what you mean. He looks like he's from my country, but I've never set eyes on him here before." The friends hung out here on most Saturday nights.

"Er… it did look like you never could take your eyes off him today. Dishy, isn't he?" Andrea fluttered her long and dark eyelashes at Dayanita, laughing too by now.

Dayanita grimaced. She wasn't going to admit that she found the man striking. Too damn attractive actually! So much so that she hadn't been able to take her eyes off him. But that didn't mean that he could check her out at will.

Jake didn't care for the turn the conversation was taking and quickly changed the subject. "So, where are we going tomorrow?" He was the only son of a millionaire film producer and didn't really understand the meaning of hard work. He believed that life was too short to keep one's nose to the grind.

"I'm going nowhere," declared Alia who was from Pakistan. "I need to call home and also have two assignments that I should have completed last week." She was the eldest child of a large family in Lahore who lived in the hope that she made it big in the US of A. While they weren't too well off, Alia had got into the course on one hundred percent scholarship.

"Me neither. I'm working tomorrow." Dino worked nearly all weekends. He was the most hardworking of the lot. His family owned several acres of flourishing vineyards in Piedmont, Italy. Being a second son, Dino was keen to carve his own path and refused to touch the pocket money that was transferred to his bank account on a monthly basis.

Before Andrea or Shawn—who originated from Brisbane, Australia—could say anything, Dayanita spoke up, "I'd love to go out tomorrow. Let's go to Universal Studios. What say? Unless you want to go somewhere else." She turned to look at Shawn and Andrea, confident that Jake would fall in with her wishes. She knew for a fact that she could twist him around her little finger without an effort. She also knew that he only lusted after her and no love was lost between the two of them.

"Okay, I'm game." Shawn nodded his blond head. He had moved to the USA four years ago, taking a well-paying job with a tech company. Finding himself bored after the first few years, he had quit his full-time job to a part-time one, funding his course at the same college the others went to.

Andrea nodded. "I'll go."

"Babe, who was that guy you were trying to beat up?" asked Shawn, turning to Dayanita.

She pouted at him. "I wasn't trying to beat him up."

Shawn laughed. "Okay. Browbeating, maybe?"

Dayanita punched him on his shoulder, her eyes twinkling merrily. "Shuddup. I'd never do that."

"Ouch!" Shawn pretended to be in pain as he grinned back at her, shaking his head. "Just that he seems familiar."

"Familiar?" Dayanita's shapely eyebrows came together in a scowl, her luscious lips taking the guise of a pout once again. "Have you been to India?"

Shawn shook his head. "Nope. Are you saying he's Indian? Do you know him?"

Dayanita shuddered. "No way. I've never seen his ugly face before."

Andrea and Alia laughed outright, ready to roll on the floor. "Ugly!" Andrea hooted. "Come on, Nita. Cut him some slack. He's one of the handsomest guys I've ever set my eyes on. And believe me, the guys from back home can be quite hot."

"I agree." Alia's black eyes danced mischievously as she studied Dayanita's face. "What's up, Nita? The guy got to you?"

"Nita likes me," Jake growled softly, his blue eyes catching fire.

Dayanita turned to raise a supercilious eyebrow at him, not saying anything when she noticed the colour run up his ruddy cheeks.

An uncomfortable silence fell over the table before all began to talk at the same time, the moment of tension lost.

It was almost two in the morning when they decided to leave, four of them finally deciding to go on a tour of Disneyland Park the next day.

"Not before 11 o' clock," insisted Dayanita. She needed her beauty sleep of at least seven hours.

Jake's driver dropped the girls at the entrance to the apartment block they lived in before taking off with the boys.

"The truth, Nita, and no less. You're attracted to that guy!" Alia declared as the girls let themselves into their first-floor rented apartment.

Dayanita couldn't stop the guilty colour that rushed up her fair cheeks as she did her best to glare at her friend, failing miserably.

"If you aren't, please tell me now. I wouldn't mind trying my luck with him." Andrea gurgled as she caught the murderous expression on Dayanita's face.

Without reponding to either of them, Dayanita walked into her bedroom and shut the door on their startled faces, before throwing her clutch across the room. It hit the opposite wall and fell down, falling open to throw up its contents. Her keys, a packet of wet-wipes, a hairbrush, a tube of lipstick and her mobile phone got strewn around the carpet. Thoroughly miffed, she went into the bathroom, pulled her clothes off before going under the shower, turning the water to hot.

She stood under the stream of water, pushing her hair out of her eyes as she stared into nothing.

That man… that man had had the audacity to laugh at her… her, Princess Dayanita Thakore of Udaipur. If only this had happened a couple of centuries ago, she would have had him drawn and quartered.

Dayanita fumed. How dared he stare at her, checking her out? She refused to admit even to herself that her eyes had wandered towards the stranger one too many times. The DJ had played a slow number and she had been dancing in Jake's arms, completely unaware of her classmate with whom she had gone to the disco. Now she remembered that Jake had buried his face in her shoulder as he took deep breaths, though at that point her focus had all been on that man at the bar.

But what the hell was she to do?! She knew that Jake lusted after her and wanted to bed her. She just wasn't interested. The six of them hung together as a gang and were good friends. That was it!

All through the twenty-six years of her life, she had not found any man she had really liked. Either they were intelligent or they were good-looking. She didn't know of any man who was both. Well, that didn't take into account her father or her brothers.

Dayanita secretly admired her father, Raja Gajendar Thakore. He was truly handsome and more than that he was extremely well-mannered. Dayanita had never openly showed her affection for her father, only because she didn't want to fall in the eyes of her grandmother, *Rajmata* Santhini Devi Thakore, who was also her father's mother. Santhini Devi didn't have a great opinion about her son.

And why did Santhini Devi dislike him? All because Gajendar loved his wife, Ragini Devi. While it was the *Rajmata* who had arranged her son's marriage to her daughter-in-law, she still did not like the idea that her son consulted his wife every time before he took a decision. Over and above that Santhini Devi thought that her timid daughter-in-law was a wimp and didn't care for the idea that she wielded such power over her son.

And the old matriarch had done her best to ingrain her thoughts into her granddaughter. While Dayanita pretended to agree with her grandmother, she had a mind of her own and knew that her father was a great man who held their family together.

Her brothers Indrajeet and Rajvardhan were truly heroes. Okay, maybe Rajvardhan could be troublesome and a tease, but at the end of the day, they would give their lives for her.

But Dayanita had never met anyone in the outside world who was as good or better than her family members.

But… Dayanita threw the damp towel angrily into the cane basket that was in one corner of the bathroom before stepping out naked into her bedroom, pulling the curtains closed at the windows.

She fell back on her bed after pulling back the comforter and lay there, staring up at the ceiling unseeingly, her mind on the man at the bar.

What was it about him that was irritating her so? She recalled his sharp features with absolute clarity. She would have expected steel grey eyes to be hard, but his had been smoky. Maybe he was into drugs and that's why his gaze was the way it was. Dayanita turned on her front to punch her pillows into shape.

It was a long time before sleep claimed her tired body.

Harshvardhan reached Disneyland a little before nine in the morning and got inside the moment the gates were thrown open to the public. This was his second visit and he was happy to be all by himself—which was a rarity.

He had walked to the amusement park from the *Mickey and Friends* parking lot and felt quite excited to be back at one of his favourite places, eating a strawberry ice-cream in a waffle cone with enthusiasm.

His first stop was at *Hyperspace Mountain*, ensuring that he had a Fast pass for the day since, being a Sunday, it was bound to be crowded with long queues for all the rides.

He had a wonderful time on the roller-coaster ride that went up and down in the darkness, hurtling through simulated space, thrilled beyond measure. It was all the more fun to be in some place where no one recognised him. He yelled his lungs off along with the others—many of them kids—who were taking the ride.

Getting off the roller-coaster, Harshvardhan walked fast to join the queue snaking towards *Big Thunder Mountain Railroad*. With a cute red engine, followed by the driver's cabin that drew open carriages behind it, the train took its passengers across the Wild West themed area, with everyone clicking away at their smart phones as they caught the diverse views of the park on their cameras.

Harshvardhan didn't notice Dayanita or her friends enter the gates of the *Haunted Mansion* only a few minutes behind him. The whole group of merrymakers entered the huge lift when the doors opened.

A sing-song male voice spoke to them, obviously doing its best to scare them off as the lift went up, the portraits on the many walls growing longer, giving an eerie effect. While children screamed—some in agony and many in laughter, the adults couldn't help laughing when they were told by the disembodied voice that there was no way to get out of the lift.

It was a few minutes before a couple of doors, opposite to the ones they had entered from, opened up to let them into the next section.

They walked along a corridor that had ghostly pictures on both sides from which lights blinked, while cobwebs hung from the ceiling. Soon, they got into the ride—C-shaped cars on rails that could hold two people at one go. Another guy who was also all by himself, joined Harshvardhan in his car.

Soon, they took off to check out the 999 ghosts— according to the voice—that haunted the mansion.

It was more fun than horrifying, thought Harshvardhan when they finally got out of the mansion. It was time to go get some food!

"You!" Dayanita stopped in her tracks to glare at her tormentor from the earlier day.

Harshvardhan had taken a couple of steps ahead before he realised that it was a familiar voice before he turned to see Ms Hoity-toity from the earlier night. Her long, slim legs were encased in a pair of short shorts in brilliant white that she had paired with a halter-neck cropped top in a brilliant shade of orange. She was truly a sight for sore eyes, her brown eyes alight with temper, before she pulled a pair of large-framed goggles down from where they had been resting on her head, covering them up. There were three other people with her, but he had eyes only for her.

"Hey!" he said, a mischievous grin splitting his handsome face in two, "we meet again."

"How dare you follow me? I'll…"

"Hello! Are you crazy or what?" Harshvardhan walked back the few steps to where she stood, the smile disappearing from his face.

"I'll report you for harassment." Dayanita threatened him, her fisted hands on her slender hips.

"For what?" Harshvardhan tilted his head backwards to look down his magnificently royal nose at her.

"Hey, wait a minute. I know who you are." Both of them paused in the middle of their argument and turned to look at Shawn who had exclaimed, staring at Harshvardhan with wonder in his eyes.

Shawn went forward and put out his hand to shake Harshvardhan's. "You are a Bollywood star.

Harvardhan Gaekwad! Am I right? I'm Shawn Williams. How do you do?"

Harvardhan shook Shawn's hand with a smile on his face, his surprise evident. "How did you know?"

"I've watched all the eight films that you have starred in," said Shawn enthusiastically. "I'm a total movie buff and especially enjoy Bollywood films." He took out a one-dollar bill from his wallet and offered it to Harshvardhan. "Could you please sign it for me?"

Dayanita fumed, not used to being ignored. And what was wrong with Shawn? She was sure that her tormentor couldn't be a famous Bollywood star. Wouldn't she have known if that were one, rather than Shawn? But then, it had been a few years since Dayanita had kept track of Bollywood films, not since she had become enamoured with Hollywood, influenced by her western friends. And moreover, she had been living abroad over the past three-plus years.

"Shall we go on?" She asked extra loudly, irritated with Shawn for fawning over the alleged film-star of Bollywood. "I'm keen to check out the *Pirates of the Caribbean.*"

For once, her friends ignored her, waiting their turns to be introduced to the actor, shaking his hand enthusiastically.

"I'm truly looking forward to your lecture tomorrow," said Shawn, smiling his enthusiasm.

"As do I. This will be the first time I'll be addressing the students at your academy."

What the hell were they talking about?

It was during lunch at *Redd Rockett's Pizza Port* that Dayanita got to know about the lecture which had been organised by the Indian students of their academy. Always preferring to know any agenda only at the last minute, she hadn't bothered to find out the programme for the next day.

"Harshvardhan Gaekwad will be addressing us at 4 pm tomorrow. I plan to reach there early, to make sure that I get into one of the first five rows." Shawn continued to wax lyrical about his favourite star as he took a bite of his pepperoni pizza, much to Dayanita's annoyance.

"Do you want to take off with me?" she asked Jake on an aside, not too keen to listen to Shawn singing Gaekwad's praises.

Even before Jake could reply, Shawn spoke to Dayanita. "Hey, did you know that Harshvardhan is also an Indian royalty? He's a prince belonging to the Baroda lineage."

Dayanita paled as the colour drained from her cheeks. "Are you sure?" Maybe Shawn had got his information all wrong. If he was right, then she had really been foolish, throwing her weight around at the man last night. Her exact words flashed before her mind's eye: *Do you know who I am?* Shucks! This was seriously embarrassing. But then, he had not retaliated with any princely airs, none that she noticed anyway.

In the end, she sat through Shawn's long talk about Harshvardhan; how he was a prince and all about how he had become a successful movie star. Jake was so obviously fascinated, same as Andrea.

Dayanita gritted her teeth until her jaws hurt. If all that Shawn said was true, she wondered that Prince Harshvardhan didn't fall down, face first, what with the excess weight of his head.

She was disgusted by the time they called it a day, more irritated than usual as she had got to sleep barely a few hours the earlier night.

And who was the cause of all her misery? None other than Prince Harshvardhan Singh Gaekwad.

She decided then and there that she would skip the man's lecture. After all, she didn't think he was really the God's gift to mankind that Shawn seemed to believe him to be.

Dayanita shut herself in her room the moment they got home, booting her laptop almost immediately. She had to know if all the information Shawn had fed them was true.

The moment she typed Harshvardhan, his images popped up on Google search, even before she began typing his surname. Posters of all eight of his every damn film came up. Dayanita refused to acknowledge that she was dying of curiosity.

Imagine that he was also a prince from a well-known royal family! She had heard about Sitara Gaekwad from her brother Rajvardhan. It looked like the woman was Harshvardhan's elder sister by six years. Dayanita ran a swift eye over the many links that came up with her tormentor's name.

After reading the topmost five links, Dayanita could understand why Shawn thought so highly of his movie idol. It looked like Harshvardhan Gaekwad had not just the public but also the media eating out of his hand.

"Uff!" Dayanita shut her laptop none too gently, getting up with a jerk, her mind recalling with crystal clarity his charcoal gaze that twinkled with mirth before turning turbulent, reminding one of storm clouds when he lost his cool.

What the fuck! Twinkled with mirth! Turbulent storm clouds! Now who the hell was waxing lyrical about the man?!

Dayanita stepped out of her room into the balcony, thoroughly irritated and restless. It was some time before she went back to sit in the middle of her bed, her chin on her drawn up knees, staring at the closed door, her mind randomly mulling over her life at the Thakore palace in Udaipur as the only princess, the youngest member of her generation.

er grandmother had told Dayanita very clearly from when she had been a child that they were royalty and the rest of the world existed to serve them, to cater to their whims and fancies.

Growing up at *Rajmata* Santhini Devi's knee, Dayanita had always grabbed what she wanted, with both hands. Despite their cash crunch while she was growing, she had never been denied anything. If anyone had borne the brunt of the lack of funds, it had been her parents to the maximum extent and then her brothers, who were both elder to her. Dayanita and her grandmother had led their lives exactly how the matriarch pleased.

Her father, Gajendar, had sold their summer palace to the hotelier Ritvik Bansal, who had converted it into a 5-star hotel called *Maharaja International*. This was the primary reason for Santhini Devi's anger towards her son.

Once they had come into the money, Gajendar had been keen to send all his three children abroad for their post-graduation. While her brothers had jumped at the chance, Santhini Devi had discouraged Dayanita from taking up the offer.

"You are a royal first, Dayanita. You are a graduate and that's enough. Now what I want you to do is to woo Ritvik Bansal into marrying you. That way, the palace will continue to remain in our family." Santhini Devi had fed the thought into young Dayanita's mind. The princess had been barely twenty then while the hotelier had been at least a decade older.

But Dayanita had always clung to her grandmother's words, even if at times that had turned her against her own mother. She had chased Ritvik, and how! While he had always treated her like a pesky kid. She had kept throwing herself at him while he managed to keep her at arms' length.

A couple of years later, Indrajeet persuaded Dayanita to grab the opportunity to study abroad. "You are young, Nita. Don't you want to have a career of your own?"

"But Jeet, Grandma says that my goal is to get married to the most suitable man..."

"And you think Ritvik is the guy? Wake up, Nita. For one thing, Ritvik is way too old for you. And for another, the world has changed from the time when Grandma was your age. Being a wife is not a full-time occupation. You are smart and did so well at college. Going abroad to study further will also be a chance to spread your wings, know more about the rest of the world. When you live in another country, you learn so much about a different culture. It will make you more independent. You..."

"But I don't want to be independent." Dayanita glared at her brother angrily. *What does he know about what I want?*

"Eh? That's crap and you know it Nita. Everyone wants to be independent," Indrajeet said forcefully.

"More than that, I want our palace to look beautiful." There was a mutinous expression on Dayanita's face. "Have you seen Ritvik's hotel? He has lavished money on the place and it looks simply gorgeous," she said wistfully.

Indrajeet gave her a hug. "I know, sweetie. Believe me, our palace will also be restored to its former glory, I promise you. But in the meanwhile, I would rather you stopped chasing Ritvik and study further."

"But there's nothing I want to study more. I find going to college and giving exams so damn boring." What Dayanita didn't put into words was that while in college, she had believed herself to be way above her classmates and had refused to mingle with any of them. In the end, the college years that should have been absolute fun, had been too lonely for the Thakore princess.

Santhini Devi's influence on her granddaughter was total and she had convinced Dayanita that as royals they were a cut above the rest of the population.

Indrajeet sighed, fairly well aware of what must have happened. For, hadn't Santhini Devi tried the same trick on him and Rajvardhan as well? While his younger brother argued and teased their grandmother, Indrajeet treated her fondly, doing exactly as he pleased.

It was Dayanita who had fallen prey to the matriarch's teachings and had turned out to be snootier than even the old lady.

"Look at it like this, Nita. Even the European royals and those from the Arabian countries go to study in American universities." He gave his sister a sly look from the corner of his eyes, seeing if his words were having the desired effect.

"Oh really?" Dayanita sat up straight on the sofa, eyeing her brother with widened eyes. "Are you sure?"

"Of course. The princess of Denmark and the prince of Sharjah are in Harvard along with me."

"What? Are you serious?" There was excitement in the young cynic's eyes as she listened avidly to her brother's words.

"*Kasam se*," he swore, his hand at his throat adding emphasis to his words and a convincing smile on his face. "Believe me, it's only the very rich and highly intelligent people who get into the university there, especially post-grad level. Even Pappa could think of sending Raj and me only after selling our summer palace. We couldn't have afforded it otherwise."

Dayanita's lips drooped, her expression turning petulant. "That was really wrong on Pappa's part," she declared, uttering the words that her grandmother had poured into her ears repeatedly.

Indrajeet's brown eyes, exactly the shade as his sister's, caught fire as he took a deep breath before saying patiently, "It wasn't Pappa's fault. He only did what needed to be done. Properties can be bought once we accumulate wealth again. But we can't stop living…"

"I don't want to hear that argument." Dayanita placed both her palms over her ears, shaking her head vigorously in protest.

Indrajeet pulled her hands away from her ears. "Listen, you little fool. I know Grandma has been filling your head about how the palace is heritage property and has been in our family since four-hundred-plus years. But what about our family history itself? When the first Thakore—Raja Pratapsinh—whom we can trace back as our earliest ancestor, began his life, he didn't have two coins to rub together. But with his hard work and loyalty to the king of this region, he was given the lands that we own today and also the title of Raja." He drew in a deep breath before continuing, "Our lands had been yielding too less over a decade. The farmers needed to be…"

"Why the hell is Pappa bothered about the farmers? They are used to being poor. Isn't it their duty to give all their yield to their ruler?" Dayanita's voice rose along with her temper. How dare he call her a fool? Just because he was elder to her by a few years didn't make Indrajeet more intelligent than she.

"What? Do you even understand what you are saying? Or are you just parroting Grandma's words?" He got up from his seat to walk up and down, agitation in every line of his body as he continued to talk. "First of all, let's be clear that we are royals in name only. We have lots of lands and two palaces left over at present. We have cash, only because we sold away the summer palace." He raised a hand to stop Dayanita when she would have interrupted. "Hear me out, fully. The farmers are human beings too. They work on the land throughout the year. Their families need to be fed, clothed and educated. And we have a responsibility towards them. They…"

Dayanita jumped up from her seat to scream, "That's utter crap. We are royalty, even today. I know that our country's a republic and all that. But we still own the damn lands. They are ours and what comes out of the lands belong to us. We..."

"And what do you think the lands are going to give us without the people working on them?" Indrajeet was standing in front of her, his hands on his hips as he glared at his sister from his superior height.

"But that's their duty. They..."

"Let's presume that we are royals. Then, don't we have a duty towards them as well?" Indrajeet was on the verge of banging Dayanita's and his grandmother's heads together to make them see sense. What the hell was the old lady feeding into the young and impressionable girl's ears?

"First and foremost, everything is for us. They can have whatever is left over." Dayanita gave him a triumphant look, confident that she knew best.

"After the kind of expenses that Grandma incurs, it's a wonder that we can have two square meals a day, let alone keep this palace warm."

"Is that what Pappa's been telling you?" She challenged, her body language aggressive.

"No." Indrajeet shook his head slowly from side to side. "That's not what Pappa has been telling me. I know it for a fact since I maintained the account books until I went away to Harvard."

Dayanita blanched, staring at her brother, horrified. "Tell me you're joking."

"No, I'm not. And before you blame Pappa for everything, the decision to sell the summer palace was taken after all of us sat together and spoke about it. Oh yes, everyone, including Grandma."

"But you guys didn't include me in the discussion."

"That was because you were not even eighteen and it would have been too traumatic for you." His voice was gentle when he spoke now, trying to pull Dayanita's resisting body into a hug.

"You mean it's not a trauma now?"

"Listen, Nita. There are so many people in our country who sleep on the roads, who don't even have one square meal in a day. They probably have just the one set of clothes that they wear. They…"

"I don't care, do you hear? I don't want to know. Why should I? I'm the Thakore princess and I wish to live like royalty. I don't want to…"

"Which is exactly why Pappa sold the palace. To help us all continue to lead a lavish life."

And they were back to square one in their argument. Dayanita scowled at Indrajeet. "You are confusing me. First, you say that people sleep on roads without food. Then you say that our palace was sold so that we can live like royalty. What the hell do you mean, Jeet?"

"That you bloody well appreciate what you have, Nita, instead of complaining about every damn thing."

She stared at him, aghast. Was that what she was doing? But even after more than two years, Grandma was too angry with their father for selling the property that had been in their family for so many centuries. How could Indrajeet justify that? She was bewildered.

"Now forget all that. Let's talk about you broadening your horizons." Indrajeet was keen to get her out from under their grandmother's influence, first and foremost. The old lady was corrupting the girl and turning her into a shrew. Getting out into the real world would definitely be an improvement to living in the palace without an agenda other than to visit the beauty salon or making Ritvik Bansal's life hell.

"But Grandma says I should marry Ritvik." The mutinous look was back on her face.

Indrajeet gave an impatient sigh. "Listen, do you even understand that marriage is a decision taken by both parties concerned? You can't simply decide to marry Ritvik. He should also be interested. He..."

"Exactly. That's why Grandma has a plan..."

"No." Indrajeet's voice was firm as he glared into his sister's eyes. "Grandma's plan isn't going to be put to action, only because it's utterly crazy. It might also help her land behind bars."

Dayanita gritted her teeth, refusing to reply to him. She felt he was simply being difficult.

Indrajeet continued, "So, I've got a lot of brochures for you to look at. Check out the different PG courses and universities today. Choose five of them and we'll talk about them tomorrow. Okay?"

"Do I have a choice?" Dayanita glared at her brother.

"You do." He patted her cheek gently. "You always do. You can choose to spread your wings and make something of yourself or you can twiddle your thumbs throughout your life. It's your call." He left the palace immediately, leaving her alone to chew on his parting shot.

Dayanita thought long and hard, checking out the brochures and also the many universities and their campuses on the internet, her excitement growing steadily when she imagined living in a strange country, among strangers. And maybe learning something new.

And then something happened, something so terrible that Dayanita was forced to see the wisdom in Indrajeet's words.

Santhini Devi's loyal servant Meghnath kidnapped Ritvik's surrogate daughter Aarya at the matriarch's instigation. All hell had broken loose. It was lucky that Indrajeet had managed to save the situation before it took a dangerous turn and Ritvik didn't have to undergo too much anguish. But it had completely put the *Rajmata's* nose out of joint.

The incident had also managed to convince Dayanita that her grandmother was not always right, making the old lady lose her death grip on her. That was also when she decided to keep away from Ritvik.

Once she accepted that it didn't make sense chasing after Ritvik, Dayanita realised that she really had nothing to do. So, with Indrajeet's guidance, she chose a few universities and set about applying to them. Soon, she had got caught up in the challenges of giving entrance exams, determined now that she got exactly what she wanted.

"So, you are going ahead with Indrajeet's idea?" There was disappointment in *Rajmata* Santhini Devi's voice as she gave her youngest grandchild a bitter look. "And here I was dreaming that you will marry Ritvik Bansal one day and bring the palace back into our family.

"Grandma, Ritvik is never going to marry me and you well know that. And I agree with Jeet that I don't want to marry anyone so early in my life. I…"

"And why not? You aren't all that young. You are twenty-three. I was barely sixteen when I married your grandfather."

Dayanita laughed, going to sit next to Santhini Devi and giving her a hug. "But Grandma, that was in those days. Nowadays, girls marry once they have made a career for themselves. I'm glad that Jeet opened my eyes to it. I'm off to Georgia and will return, armed with a PG certificate."

"Whatever! I hope for your sake that it will be of some use to you." Santhini Devi glared at Dayanita. The old matriarch would never admit to anyone that she was going to miss her granddaughter and protégée.

A sigh shuddered through Dayanita's being when she came back to the present. That had been four years ago. Today, at twenty-seven, she was almost done with her studies abroad and couldn't wait to get back home. She swore to herself that she wasn't going to let the likes of Harshvardhan bother her.

But even then, it was almost four in the morning before sleep finally claimed her.

4

In the end, bombarded by all her friends, Dayanita didn't really have a chance but to attend Harshvardhan's lecture.

The MC took the mike to introduce the actor. With an expression of complete boredom, Dayanita sat in the third row—where Shawn had managed to snag seats—along with her friends. She refused to admit to the surprise she felt when she saw that the auditorium with a capacity for two thousand people was full, with more students standing against the walls.

Was the man genuinely popular or was it the aura of a Bollywood star? She turned her gaze from the crowd up to the dais and looked at Harshvardhan. He was dressed in a natty suit of pearl grey, teamed with a white shirt, along with a bow-tie and cummerbund of a brilliant shade of royal blue. He looked dashing to put it mildly. He wore his hair a couple of inches longer than was formal, the strands reaching down to his muscular shoulders. It was brushed back neatly and away from the broad forehead and dark eyebrows that framed his large eyes that appeared to be minutely studying the crowd. There was nothing to suggest from his body language that he was even a tad nervous at seeing such a huge turnout. But then, he was probably used to such adulating crowds.

Dayanita pouted. Big deal! Just then, she found her gaze caught by those grey eyes that had been giving her sleepless nights. He smiled, setting the blood soaring straight up to her head as she lost her cool. Who the hell did he think he was? Jerking her head in the other direction, she pulled her gaze from his with an effort to concentrate on what the Master of Ceremonies was saying, almost immediately wishing that she hadn't.

The man was listing all of Harshvardhan's achievements since the day he had decided to join Bollywood. Fascinated despite herself, though she would have never admitted to it even at gunpoint, Dayanita tilted her head to the left as she listened to every word. It seemed as if Harshvardhan's path to stardom hadn't been a bed of roses. He had had to struggle just like everyone else who didn't belong to the film fraternity or wasn't from one of the famous Bollywood families.

So, what's the big deal? She mentally shrugged, *that's how it was out there in the real world, for everyone.*

Just as she wondered if Harshvardhan's words would be as interesting as his acting career graph, she mentally paused to hear the MC's next words. "I call Princess Dayanita Thakore, a real princess, also from India, to the stage, to present a bouquet of flowers to our guest speaker, His Royal Highness Prince Harshvardhan Singh Gaekwad."

With everyone clapping loudly, Dayanita got up from her chair to walk out of the row and up the steps to the dais, a dazed expression on her face. Her legs were trembling, but that was only because it was sudden and unexpected, the MC calling out to her. It had nothing to do with the fact that she was walking closer to her tormentor.

This, she had never expected. Why the hell hadn't someone warned her about it? Wasn't it a good thing that she had decided to wear a light silk sari for the programme instead of the ragged jeans that she had originally planned to? And that was only because she had received a message on the college WhatsApp group regarding the Indian ethnic dress code for the evening.

She wasn't to know that the girl who had been given the task of presenting the bouquet had suddenly taken ill and hadn't been able to make it to the programme.

Harshvardhan looked at the beautiful woman walking up the steps onto the stage. Despite the irritated expression on her face, she looked lovely. The aquamarine silk of the sari draped over her slim figure, made her appear more graceful than ever. The heavily embroidered halter neck blouse of the same shade clung to her breasts, following the shape snugly, drawing one's eye to the shadowy cleavage on display. Her face was lightly and perfectly made up while heavy chandelier earrings of sapphires set in gold swung from her ears every time she moved her head.

He got up from his chair when she walked up to him with a huge bouquet of white lilies in her arms, his eyes running over her avidly.

"Hello!" Harshvardhan smiled at her.

"Hello yourself! Welcome to our film academy," she said politely, her eyes a fiery brown as they shot sparks at him.

He accepted the bouquet from her, his hands deliberately touching hers. What he didn't expect were the sparks of electricity that ran through his fingers when they came in contact with her skin. He received the bouquet and shifted a couple of inches away from her, startled by his own reaction.

"Thank you, Princess Dayanita Thakore," he said, his eyes gleaming mischievously. "Now I know who you are." His voice turned softer, the last words for her ears alone.

Dayanita glared at him, gritting her teeth. Her hands felt as if they had been burned by his touch. What the hell!

"I'd advise you to chill, real princess." There was laughter in his voice. "Cameras are sensitive and capable of catching every nuance in your expression."

If looks could kill, Harshvardhan would have dropped down dead at that very moment.

Dayanita swallowed her pride with difficulty before saying, "Looking forward to hearing your lecture, Your Royal Highness. I wouldn't want to keep your eager audience waiting anymore."

Just when she would have left the stage, the MC insisted that she wait for photographs while camera bulbs flashed from all across the hall. The Prince of Baroda and the Princess of Udaipur were both caught in the same frame, multiple times over.

"And now I give you the Bollywood star Harshvardhan Gaekwad…"

With a thunderous applause, Harshvardhan took to the podium. Over the next couple of hours, he enthralled the audience with his talk, before throwing open the floor for questions.

Over the next hour and fifteen minutes, a number of students asked him numerous questions and he answered them all with both intelligence and patience.

Dayanita sat through it all, the backs of her hands still tingling from his touch. And his voice—that rich baritone—seemed to ring in her ears, creating goose bumps over her skin. Generally cynical about everything, she couldn't find one single fault with his speech. He really seemed to be aware of the pulse of the audience and spoke accordingly.

The best was saved for the last.

"So, I have an offer for you guys. At the end of your course, the best three scripts that your academy selects may be sent to me. I promise to find producers for those films." The audience roared its approval as all came to their feet as one, clapping non-stop over the next few minutes.

During the gala dinner hosted by the students' council, everyone got to interact with the star. Dayanita did her best to stay as far away from Harshvardhan as possible, highly disturbed by her own reaction to him. She tried to eat from the plate that Jake brought for her, only to find her throat all choked up.

"That was the best lecture I've heard in a long time." Andrea smiled widely, pulling up the sliding *dupatta* on her left shoulder for the nth time. She was dressed in a *salwar suit* that she had borrowed from Dayanita, looking elegant.

"Tell me about it," said Alia, sipping from a can of Pepsi.

Shawn had such a smug expression on his face. "I'm going to win this contest."

"What contest?" Dayanita glared at him, a deep scowl on her forehead. She felt he was being over enthusiastic about the whole scene.

"The one that Harsh announced regarding the scripts. I plan to bag a chance to have mine made into a Bollywood film." There were stars in Shawn's eyes as he grinned at his friends.

From when had Harshvardhan become Harsh? Dayanita gave Shawn an angry look.

Jake stood back, a bored expression on his face. He realised that Dayanita didn't think too much of the actor and it suited him well as he wanted her attention all on himself. He felt on fire as he noticed her almost bare back with a small strip of cloth in the middle that held her blouse in place. She looked even more delicious from the front, the amount of cleavage that showed making him want to drool. He had been having a difficult time keeping his hands to himself as her right breast encased in the sea-green blouse with bold red and black embroidery seemed to invite his touch.

Dino joined the melee, his plate loaded with pasta and lamb chops. "I spoke to the man himself. For such a big star, he sure has no airs."

Dayanita was tired of hearing Harshvardhan's praise by now. "Excuse me, guys. I'll see you soon." She almost ran on her way to the washroom.

Just as she would have escaped, an all-too-familiar voice stopped her. "Where are you off to, real princess?"

"Will you stop calling me that?" Dayanita stopped in her tracks to turn around and snarl at Harshvardhan.

He raised his hands defensively in front of him, dragging his gaze with difficulty from her cleavage up to her face. "You look gorgeous, Princess Dayanita."

The sincerity in his expression threw her even as hot colour rushed up her cheeks. Too stunned to have a comeback, Dayanita simply looked up at him, mesmerised by the glow in his charcoal gaze.

"Have lunch with me tomorrow?" Harshvardhan spoke softly.

"Huh!" Dayanita shook her head, still dazed by his unexpected words and behaviour. "I have classes…"

"Dinner then?"

Her long, curling eyelashes fluttered as Dayanita made an effort to get back to her normal and haughty self. An inherently feminine softness—unheard of before now—seemed to become her downfall. "Er… I…"

He smiled softly, his whole face lighting up. "I'd like to know you more." His voice was softer than ever, a whisper by now, his gaze intent as they looked deeply into her eyes.

Dayanita gave him a small nod, too choked to speak.

"I'm honoured, Princess Dayanita. May I have your contact number please?"

He was polite too! She gave it to him, incapable of refusing him by now.

The next minute a group of students surrounded Harshvardhan and the two of them got separated.

Dayanita almost ran towards the washroom and hid herself in a toilet, her chest heaving as she took deep breaths, hoping to calm down her wildly beating heart. What had happened just now? Had she agreed to have dinner with her tormentor? The man who was responsible for not one, but two sleepless nights in a row?

Have I gone mad? Dayanita asked herself, her mind whirling in confusion. But her heart didn't seem to care as it insisted on looking forward to spending the next evening with Prince Harshvardhan. Torn between her mind and heart, Dayanita ran away from the party scene altogether, unable to face the revelry anymore.

Harshvardhan kept staring at the doorway through which Dayanita had disappeared, waiting for her to return. While he continued to chat with the eager students, his eyes kept a lookout for her. It was after about half an hour when he reached the conclusion that she was not going to come back to the party. The evening did not seem as interesting any more after the disappearance of the Thakore princess. Soon, he made his escape after waving to everyone on his way out.

Taking out his phone, he sent Dayanita a message.

Missed U princess. Whr hv U dsprd to?

Harshvardhan smiled when two blue ticks appeared almost immediately, and he waited eagerly for her reply.

Jst beat. Gnite

He sighed, still smiling as he wished her goodnight. A princess with an attitude! He was definitely attracted to her. He looked forward to their dinner date tomorrow, still finding it difficult to believe that she had agreed to go out with him in the first place.

Harshvardhan returned to his garden suite at The Beverly Hills Hotel in a happy frame of mind. He removed his clothes the moment he entered his bedroom before walking into the en suite bathroom.

He stood under the lukewarm shower, his mind not really on it as he kept thinking of Dayanita, the real princess. He grinned to himself. That term sure seemed to get under her skin. What had really surprised him was how she had so easily agreed to have dinner with him the next day.

Harshvardhan towelled himself dry before wrapping one of the towelling robes around his muscular body as he stepped back into his bedroom.

Pulling on a pair of shorts and a sleeveless vest before tucking his feet into a pair of moccasins, he opened the French windows and went into the garden, taking a walk. It was so quiet and beautiful in the hotel's garden, away from the swimming pool. The fragrance of oranges hit his nostrils as he took a deep breath, savouring the atmosphere. He walked for half an hour before returning to his suite, sitting down to read from one of the scripts he had brought along with him.

The visit to Los Angeles had happened in-between films. He preferred to take at least a two-week break before prepping for the forthcoming project, a kind of me-time that he used for travelling and reading. He had booked one of the best suites at The Beverly Hills Hotel once his lecture at the Los Angeles Film Academy had been confirmed. Despite the renovations going on in the hotel, it was the perfect place to rest and recuperate.

It was past three in the morning when Harshvardhan completed the script he was reading before going to sleep.

Dayanita turned around to lie down on her stomach, her right arm curled around her pillow. Nope! Sleep just refused to come and this was the third night in a row. What the hell was happening? Why couldn't she get the arrogant man out of her mind?

Harshvardhan's strong features seemed to have embedded themselves behind her eyelids, making her eyes burn with… what? Dayanita knew not. She simply hated the idea that she couldn't stop thinking about him. Granted that he was handsome. But then, so were many men, not just in India but in the US too. Dayanita had come across way better-looking men during her lifetime. Then what was it about Harshvardhan that she felt such a morbid fascination for him?

She couldn't deny that he was smart. Only an intelligent mind could have given that speech at the film academy. And it wasn't as if he had been reading from his phone. It had sounded too natural and he had been brilliant and quick-witted while answering so many questions from the students, not once sounding repetitive.

And his bearing was royal, no doubt, being from the present generation of a royal lineage that went back by at least three centuries.

But then, she herself was also from a royal family that was more than four centuries old. So, what was the big deal about Prince Harshvardhan Singh Gaekwad for her to lose sleep over?

Dayanita was stumped! She got up suddenly to look for the remote before adjusting the air-conditioner to a cooler temperature. She refused to acknowledge that she was feeling hot just thinking about the man, her flesh standing up in goose bumps.

Why the fuck had she agreed to have dinner with him? He must have mesmerised her into it. How else?

She had been truly impressed by his lecture, despite herself. Later, when he had asked her out, her mind had simply gone blank. Dayanita shook her head to herself. This just wouldn't do. If he could do that to her in a hall where more than two thousand people had been present, what would happen if they sat to an intimate dinner for two at a fine dine restaurant?

She shuddered. No way! No way was she going to let him wield that kind of an influence over her. What should she do? Maybe send him a message that she won't be able to make it? She could plead a prior appointment which she had forgotten about. But that would show her in an unfavourable light, as if she tended to forget things, which was so not true.

Or worse, that he made her forget things. *That,* would never do.

But whatever her excuse was, it wouldn't work in the long run. He might simply ask her out again. And no, she didn't think it was a good idea to spend private time with Harshvardhan. In the three times she had encountered him, she had spent—was spending—as many sleepless nights. And she had quarrelled with him each time. She shuddered to think of the effect a dinner date with the prince would have on her.

How should she handle it then? Dayanita decided that it would be for the best if she simply stood him up. That was it. They were supposed to meet at a downtown restaurant at 7.30 pm. She would simply not turn up for the date.

Coming to the decision, she punched her pillows for the tenth time, laying her head on them, waiting for the elusive sleep to claim her, which it did at around five in the morning.

6

When Dayanita didn't turn up for their dinner date on time, Harshvardhan sent her many WhatsApp messages. But to his disappointment, the ticks remained grey, refusing to turn blue. He waited till eight before giving her a call only to find her phone switched off by then.

What the fuck!

It didn't strike him that she had stood him up. Being a handsome, rich and famous film-star as well as a royal prince—even in an independent country—at that, many women would have given an arm and a leg to date Harshvardhan. There was no dearth of feminine company whether he was back home or travelling abroad. This was the first time he had wanted to date a particular woman. But where the hell was she?

A small frown gathered on his forehead as he sipped from his glass of Scotch and soda. Could something bad have happened? Dayanita had agreed to meet him here for dinner. If she had changed her mind or just in case something had come up, she would have definitely informed him. But there was no such message from her.

Her heart began to beat heavily as a sudden thought came to his mind. What in case she had had an accident? He placed a hand against the left side of his chest to calm himself down. He was getting paranoid. Taking a deep breath, he called Shawn.

"Hey mate! How have you been?" Shawn greeted Harshvardhan enthusiastically.

"I'm good. And you?"

"Amazing, mate. We were all just talking about you. We're here at Exchange LA once again today. Why don't you join us? If you're free, that is?"

If something had happened to Dayanita, her closest friends wouldn't be club-hopping, would they? Something within Harshvardhan pushed him to accept Shawn's invitation. It was forty-five minutes since their appointed time. Somehow, he didn't think the real princess was going to show up after all this long.

"I'll see you there in a bit. Thanks, Shawn." Harshvardhan's jaw was granite hard when he paid for his drinks before leaving the restaurant, tipping the *maître d'* heavily and requesting him to keep the table free just in case. He got into the hotel's car that he had hired for the evening and directed the driver to take him to the night club. Would Dayanita be there? Well, it won't be long before he got to know the truth.

Dayanita sat quietly at the table for six, sipping on her cocktail. While she had been determined to thwart Harshvardhan's attempt to spend time with her, she couldn't help the feeling of disappointment that dogged her. She would have liked to know him more. Jake had gone out with someone else while the other four of her friends had been planning to hang out at the club for the evening. Not keen to sit by herself at home, she had decided to join them at the last minute and here she was. The four of them were dancing. Since it was not really a couple dance, she could have easily joined them. Only she wasn't in the mood for it.

She tilted her head to toss the drink back into her throat when she noticed Harshvardhan step into the disco, the psychedelic lights playing over his arrogant features. Her heart stopped beating for a few seconds, almost suffocating her before it began to beat at double pace. Was it a coincidence that the prince was here just now?

She stared at him with a heavy scowl on her face as he walked towards her, having caught sight of her.

Was he glad that he had caught her alone! "I thought we had a dinner date." Harshvardhan's voice was a growl as he pulled the chair next to hers before plonking down on it.

She looked him up and down. He was even handsomer than the earlier day at the academy, wearing a pale blue linen jacket over a white tee, teamed with designer jeans. Damn him! Why did he have to look so good every time she set eyes on him?

"Damn it! Are you going to even answer me?" His grey eyes blazed darkly, sending a zing of thrill down her spine.

"Er… umm… I…"

"All you had to tell me was that you didn't want my company. Would that have been so difficult?" His voice was a snarl now as he gave her a furious look.

"Hey mate! You made it." Shawn's voice interrupted them as he sat next to Harshvardhan, giving him a friendly slap on his back.

"Shawn," said Harshvardhan, his voice mellowing even as he smiled. "Yeah, and thanks to you. I was at a loose end since my date stood me up."

"What?" Andrea stared at the movie star. "I refuse to believe it. Who's this idiot? I wish I had known before. I'd have joined you for dinner." She smiled at him, open admiration on her face.

"And I'd have been honoured, lovely Andrea." Harshvardhan openly flirted with the Greek woman, setting Dayanita's teeth on edge.

She looked at the three of them—Harshvardhan, Shawn and Andrea. Talk about being saved by a hair's breadth! The other two had arrived in the nick of time. She had been totally flummoxed as to what to say to Harshvardhan. She couldn't very well tell him that she had decided to stand him up. Of all the rotten luck! Why did Shawn have to invite the man over today?

"Would you like to dance, Princess Dayanita?" Harshvardhan's steely gaze was fixed on hers as he asked her politely. Only she knew that it was an order cloaked in a request for the others' sake.

Dayanita got up with reluctance. She wasn't keen to be grilled. But it looked like she didn't really have a choice but to go face the music.

Harshvardhan placed a hard arm around her slender waist as the DJ played a slow number much to Dayanita's irritation. He took her slender right hand in his left, holding it up at her shoulder level, his steely gaze like a lance as he looked into her stormy brown eyes. "You owe me an explanation."

"No, I don't. I can see that you would have been happy with just about anybody for your dinner date, since you mentioned that you'd have been honoured to have gone out with Andrea." Offence was the best way of defence. That's what Dayanita decided in the few moments it had taken them to reach the dance floor from their table.

"What?! Did you just hear yourself?" Harshvardhan frowned as he looked down at the rebellious expression on her face. "Tell me something, *real princess*." His voice was heavily sarcastic as he called her by the nickname he had given her. "Did you by any chance feel compelled to accept my invitation last evening? You could have just said 'no', couldn't you?"

She looked into his eyes for a moment before her eyelids came down to hide the expression in her eyes. With difficulty, she curbed the sigh that wanted to burst forth from within her. How she wished that she had said 'no'! He would not understand. Somehow, yesterday, after being so impressed by him, she had thought that she would like to get to know him better. But that had been before she tossed and turned on her bed for the third night in a row. And it was all because of him. She simply could not allow another human being to have so much power over her, especially someone from the opposite sex.

Harshvardhan gave her a disgusted look when there was no answer forthcoming. But as he kept looking at her, his expression changed as he became fascinated by her beauty. She was wearing jeans and a simple, sleeveless top while her hair was loose, falling down to her waist. Even her make-up was minimal, as if she had left her home in a hurry.

"Is there a problem, Nita?" he asked, his voice having lost its sting as his gaze turned gentle. He couldn't remain angry with her for long.

The sigh that had been kept under tight control whooshed out of Dayanita's chest. She looked up into his eyes, finding herself drowning in their grey depths. She began to shake her head before changing her mind and nodding at him.

Harshvardhan grinned, making her breath catch in her throat. "So, is there a problem or no?"

"I don't know what to say." Her voice came in a whisper and he had to bend down close to her mouth to hear her words.

"Okay. Let's forget what happened earlier. I've still not had dinner. Have you?"

Her heart thumped harder than ever as she shook her head firmly this time. "No."

"Would you like to go have dinner with me? And," he raised his hand to stop her from answering, "you can say 'no' if you don't wanna go with me." A dark eyebrow rose up to touch his hairline as he gave her an amused look. What he refused to make obvious was the need he felt to gather her in his arms and kiss her luscious mouth deeply and mercilessly.

Dayanita's lips parted in a soft smile, making his blood pressure go up by several notches. "I'd like to go. The truth is that I'm hungry and I would like to eat a substantial meal rather than the snacks they serve here."

He threw back his head and laughed uproariously. "*Chalo*, glad to know that I do have my uses. Let's go."

They waved to the others before Dayanita left with her tormentor, throwing caution to the winds. *What can happen at the worst? She would probably spend one more sleepless night.*

"Is there anywhere specific that you would like to go?" asked Harshvardhan as they waited for the driver to bring the car to the entrance of the night club.

Dayanita grimaced at him. "I'm too casually dressed. Should we go to a fast-food joint?"

He shook his head as his grey eyes ran over her slender figure in the jeans and figure-hugging top, his gaze heating up with a desire that he seemed to have no control over. "I still have the table booking at Osteria Mozza. I dare you to go there with me in the clothes you're wearing," he challenged her, amusement replacing the need in his gaze.

Her eyes turned to a shade of hot caramel as mischief lit them up. "I love Italian food. Let's go."

So, they walked into the restaurant, her hand on his elbow. He appeared suave and handsome in his smart casuals while she looked heartbreakingly beautiful in her casuals. Several heads of both men and women turned to look at the couple walking through the length of the restaurant all the way to the back where the private table that Harshvardhan had reserved for the evening stood waiting for them.

He plied her with wine, determined to know why she had not kept their appointment. She drank several glasses, keeping a cool head as she refused to give him a reason. Whatever she said was bound to sound stupid. And she definitely didn't want him to know that he was giving her sleepless nights.

The real princess could hold her drink, it seemed. She must have drunk a little more than half a bottle of the red Bordeaux wine that he had ordered with their meal and she could still chat very comfortably with him about world politics and football. It seemed that she knew a lot about Hollywood films and TV shows as well.

"I must admit that I haven't seen Bollywood films since I moved to the USA. That's why..."

Harshvardhan was captivated as he noted the colour run up her silky cheeks. He grinned, completing her sentence, "...you didn't know that I existed."

She pouted at him, not saying anything. Well, what to say! He had said it all. She really hadn't known that he existed. While Shawn, who had never been anywhere near India, knew all about Harshvardhan being a famous actor.

"I plan to watch all your films. I..."

"Let me send you a private link with a password. You can access my films from there. That is, if you really want to. Let it not be said that I twisted your arm into watching my films," he said, tongue firmly tucked in his cheek as he looked into her eyes with a mischievous glint in his own.

Her cheeks seemed to be permanently on fire as she turned red yet again. She had not expected him to be such a tease. She had never tolerated anyone teasing her before. But Harshvardhan was so gentle that she simply couldn't take offence.

It was past midnight when Harshvardhan left Dayanita outside her apartment door. "Thank you for the wonderful dinner." She was breathless as she uttered those words, her gaze clinging to his.

"And thank you for the scintillating company," he said, his voice a soft whisper as he reached forward to kiss her soft cheek. "Goodnight."

Dayanita stared after him, a hand on her cheek, shaken by the chaste kiss. But he hadn't bothered to ask her out again. After the way they had got along, she had been sure that he would have suggested that they meet again. After all, he planned to remain in Los Angeles for ten more days. And she had been looking forward to it. She was startled by the deep sense of disappointment she felt.

Will she get to meet Harshvardhan again? It was no surprise that she spent one more sleepless night all thanks to the prince of Baroda.

7

Classes were done for the day. Over the past half an hour, Dayanita had been toying with the idea of asking Harshvardhan out on a date. Where was it written that only guys should ask girls out? What was wrong if she did the asking? Putting thought into action, she sent a WhatsApp message to Star Prince as she had saved Harshvardhan's number on her phone:

R u free ths evng?

It depends

She saw the smiley face he had added next to the two words.

Dinner?

Would he agree to go with her?

Hehe if u r sur

Phew! She couldn't help but admire him for that reply.

U cn pck me up if u wnt

She added a winky emoticon to that.

Dne. Wht tme?

7

Ok

Dayanita made an extra effort to get ready for her dinner date with Harshvardhan, beginning with a long soak in the lavender scented bath. By the time she was done, she looked like a freshly minted gold coin.

Alia opened the door when the doorbell rang exactly at seven. "Harsh, hi. Welcome to our home." She gave him a cheerful smile, opening the door wider to let him in. "My, my, isn't someone so lucky!" she said, eyeing the huge bouquet that he carried of dewy carnations in the softest of pinks. Turning around, she called out, "Nita, come along and see who's here."

Harshvardhan walked into the tastefully furnished living room and took a sofa when Alia waved him to it. He got up almost immediately when Dayanita walked out of her bedroom, his eyes wide as he stared at her.

She was dressed in a strapless silk concoction that floated down to her ankles, the pastel pink the exact shade as the carnations that Harshvardhan had brought. As the two of them stared at each other in astonishment, Alia gave a squeal of delight.

"I don't believe this. The carnations go so perfectly with your dress."

Harshvardhan simply stared, having lost his tongue, his eyes taking in her hair coiled into a knot at the top of her crown, a few silky tendrils having escaped and falling artfully down the sides of her cheeks. Her face was perfectly made up, a touch of silver eyeshadow and mascara adding mystery to her caramel brown eyes. Her cheeks were flushed naturally while her pouting lips sported a darker shade of pink than her dress.

An oval shaped, uncut pink tourmaline, the size of a pigeon's egg, was set in a silver pendant that graced the hollow in her throat where it hung from a silver chain. Matching gems set in the same design hung from silver hooks from her earlobes.

Harshvardhan didn't miss the silver armlet on her left arm, also set with three of the semi-precious stones. In the four-inch silver stilettos that completed her ensemble, she looked exactly like the princess that she was, having descended from an old royal lineage.

But how come the princess was clothed in such a long dress? The two times he had met her before the lecture at her college, she had worn such short clothes. Harshvardhan's frown cleared up the next second, his gaze turning dark with desire when she took another step forward and her dress parted at the single slit that reached up to mid-thigh.

Sensing the sizzling heat quotient in the hallway, Alia made herself scarce as she stepped out of the hall into her room.

He doesn't look so bad, thought Dayanita as she studied Harshvardhan in turn. No, she wasn't going to admit to even herself that he appeared not just dashing but arrogant as well in his coal black three-piece suit teamed with a dark red tie. Rubies winked on the gold tie-pin and in the gold cufflinks that he wore on his pristine white shirt. His longish hair was brushed back neatly while his face was clean shaven, making his jaw appear rock hard, ending in a square chin with a decided cleft. But it was his dark grey eyes that captured her attention completely. Today, they weren't smoky but totally alert as they looked her up and down.

It was Dayanita who recovered first. "Hi," she said, a trifle breathless.

"You're looking even more beautiful, Princess Dayanita," he said, giving her the bouquet, "and these are for you."

"They look lovely," said Dayanita, smiling, even as gentle colour flared up her silky soft cheeks. "Why don't you sit down? Shall I get you something to drink?"

"I'd rather we left if you're ready." He raised a thick and dark brow in query.

Dayanita nodded. "Let me put these flowers in a vase and get my clutch."

She was back within five minutes holding a silver clutch, and the two of them left. She was surprised that they could chat comfortably with each other, especially after the turbulent start.

"So, where would you like to go?" Harshvardhan asked, gunning the engine of the car he had hired from his hotel.

"I was thinking of Bar Nineteen12…"

"…at The Beverly Hills Hotel?" he laughed softly, taking off at speed.

A scowl marred Dayanita's neat forehead when she glared at him. "What's so funny?"

He shook his head, giving her a smile. "Not funny funny. Only that I'm staying at the hotel."

"Oh!" Her eyes went wide as she stared at him. He must be damned rich to be able to afford that, unless some production house was footing his bill. "Do you want to go elsewhere then?"

"No, Nineteen12 is fine."

They chatted desultorily while the ride lasted. By the time they reached his hotel, she said, "Isn't Dayanita a mouthful? You must call me Nita," with a smile on her face. Yes, it was the second time they were going on a date, but it had taken this long for the prickly princess to feel comfortable enough with Harshvardhan to say that.

A tasty mouthful indeed! It looked like the real princess had indeed thawed towards him. "Nita." He nodded. "And you should call me Harsh."

A hotel attendant opened the passenger door to let Dayanita out even before Harshvardhan got out of the driver's seat. He walked forward to take her hand to place it on his arm before the two of them stepped into the foyer.

They walked through the bar and out into the terrace which was further down, with a view of the garden and Beverly Hills beyond. They sat down on two comfortable single sofas that faced each other, set close to the wooden railing. "This place is famous for its sunsets," said Harshvardhan, taking the seat opposite hers.

"Yeah, I've heard of that." Jake had told her so many times, inviting her to go with him. But she didn't want to go on a date with Jake, only he refused to accept that.

"So, is this your first time here?" he asked, taking the menu the waiter offered.

She nodded. "Yes."

"What would you like to have?" Harshvardhan handed the drinks menu to her.

"*Long Island Iced Tea* if you have it," she said promptly to the waiter, not bothering to look into the menu.

"And I'll have a Scotch and soda, large," said Harshvardhan.

"Anything to eat, sir, madam?"

"Not for me," said Dayanita.

"Maybe later," said Harshvardhan, dismissing the waiter with a nod.

"Cheers!" he said some time later, raising his glass to her in a toast.

"Cheers!" responded Dayanita, before taking a sip from her glass. "This is perfect," she said, smacking her lips, drawing Harshvardhan's gaze to her mouth without meaning to.

He smiled, taking a sip of his drink.

"So, what's your next project? Have you signed one yet?" Dayanita was interested in knowing about his work. She planned to see all his films now that Harshvardhan had sent her the private link and password.

"Yep. Shooting begins next week."

"Oh!" So, he would be gone soon. Making an effort to hold the smile on her face, she asked, "Where?"

"I'll prep for a couple of weeks in Mumbai. After that, shooting will happen in Karjat, a hill station not far from Mumbai, over one month. Then we'll be going to Jodhpur for the next segment for forty days. A couple of songs will be shot in South Africa." He shrugged, drawing her gaze to his broad shoulders.

"Sounds like fun."

"You can say that. It's also a lot of work, though I love doing what I do."

She nodded. "I'm sure. And what about your palace and lands? Who manages them? Your family…?"

Harshvardhan's face darkened as he turned to look at the garden, his gaze on the faraway hills. "Would you like another of those?" he asked, nodding at her near-empty glass.

"Definitely, yes. This is the best *Long Island iced tea* I've ever tasted."

His melancholic expression changed when he smiled, beckoning to the waiter for a repeat order of their drinks.

With an indrawn breath, Dayanita lifted her gaze to his and saw the desire sparking there. But she reminded herself that he hadn't bothered to answer her question.

Harshvardhan answered her question belatedly. "My parents are no more. I have a sister—Sitara Devi—who's six years elder to me. She's divorced and manages all things that need to be done at the palace." He spoke quickly and succinctly, with no expression on his face, as if he wanted to get it out of the way before they could talk about something else.

Dayanita had a number of questions, but she didn't really think it was the right time to ask them.

Before she could say anything more, he spoke. "And how about you? Where to after you complete this course?" He knew she had another two months to go before she got her certificate.

"Back home to Udaipur. I can't wait to return. I love living in our palace, especially after my brother Indrajeet had it renovated to its former glory."

"Hmm. And who else is there at home?"

"My grandmother, *Rajmata* Santhini Devi; my parents, Gajendar and Ragini; Indrajeet, his wife Yashodhara who is the Jadeja princess, and their baby son, Aditya." Dayanita smiled reminiscently, recalling the baby whom she had seen when he was barely ten days old and that had been eight months ago, just before she joined the film academy. "And then there's Rajvardhan who's elder to me by two years and his wife Chitrangada, the Vasudeva princess."

"Rajvardhan Thakore! Could that be the international polo player you are talking about?" he asked, an eyebrow up in enquiry.

She nodded, a smile on her face.

"That's quite a family you have," said Harshvardhan, a trace of envy in his voice. A big family must be full of fun and laughter. Unlike his own, with just his sister and himself. There wasn't much to laugh about in their lives, though Sitara *di* and he were really close.

"Yeah." Dayanita wrinkled her nose, drawing his gaze to that feature. "It's wonderful most of the time.

But there are times when I wish to be all by myself. Oh, by the way, we have a horde of servants too."

"But then, you will need them to maintain your huge palace, right?"

She nodded. But that didn't mean she had to like having so many people under her feet. She didn't voice her thoughts though. Today, Harshvardhan was lucky to see the sweet side of her. She had decided to keep the tartness locked away for the evening.

"How big is your palace?" he asked, curious to know everything about her.

"Big enough. We have retained twenty rooms for the family. The rest of it, say about ninety percent, is for public viewing, at a cost, of course. After the taxes and everything, there's more than enough left to maintain the place."

Harshvardhan nodded, listening raptly. That's what he had been trying to convince Sitara *di* about, to throw open the palace to the public. Being the private person that she was, she hadn't shown any enthusiasm for the idea so far.

"What about yours?" Dayanita wanted to know.

"We live in the palace in Baroda, at least my sister lives there throughout the year. I visit on and off, spending a couple of days now and again. We each of us have a suite of rooms. Besides that, we keep the main hall, the dining area and the kitchen functional. The rest of the palace is shut up and the furniture all covered up." Sometimes it felt rather sad. But then, there was no sense in keeping the whole place open, especially with him living in Mumbai most of the time. It was definitely a white elephant and while the Gaekwads had pots of money, it didn't make sense throwing it all away. There was also a smaller palace in the port town of Hazira, that was kept locked up. He fondly remembered those times when the four of them—his parents, sister and he—as a family, used to go there two-three months in a year. The Tapti river was simply beautiful and he recalled the many boat trips on the river.

"Oh, but it must be lonely for her." Dayanita couldn't help exclaiming.

The light in Harshvardhan's eyes dimmed. Forgetting his manners, he got up abruptly to walk restlessly down the terrace, not saying anything in response. Sometimes, he felt terribly guilty about not being there for his sister all the time. But it had been Sitara who had egged him on to take up acting since she knew how passionate he felt about it. He took an about turn and noticed Dayanita watching him from her seat. He quickly walked back and sat down in front of her. "I'm sorry. And you're right. Sitara *di* does get lonely though she's not one to complain," he said softly.

Dayanita nodded, not saying anything, realising that she had touched a sensitive spot. They sat quietly to watch the sunset, sipping from their glasses leisurely, just relishing each other's company.

"I thought we'll have dinner in my suite, unless you're keen to go to the restaurant." Harshvardhan looked at her in enquiry.

Dayanita shrugged her delicate shoulders, the light catching the pearly sheen of her skin, the tempo of her heartbeat increasing as excitement played football in her stomach. "Dinner in your suite works for me," she said, her voice hoarse due to a throat gone dry.

Harshvardhan had to calm himself down to walk at an even gait, his footsteps matching hers while what he actually wanted to do was hold her hand in his and race across the foyer to his room. They finally got there before he opened it with his electronic key, letting her walk in ahead of him.

"This is lovely and so comfy," she said, looking at the entrance hall.

"I have to agree. It's something like a home away from home."

Harshvardhan was from a royal family that had no dearth of funds while Dayanita, despite always having lived in a palace, knew what it was not to have cash in the bank. It was only over the past few years that the Thakores had come into a lot of money, what with her father selling one of their palaces.

And it was all because of that money that she and her brothers had got the opportunity to study abroad. While she had done her Masters in English at UGA— University of Georgia—she had realised during that time that she would like to learn script-writing. And that's how she had landed at the Los Angeles Film Academy to do the one-year course on the same.

"Have a seat. Would you like another of your favourite drink? Only I'll make it for you this time," he said, walking to the well-stocked bar.

Dayanita nodded, her eyes going wide with surprise as she watched him pick all the ingredients swiftly, setting up a mixer like an experienced bartender.

Harshvardhan switched on the music system and the sound of jazz played softly in the background as he mixed the cocktail.

"Here you go." Harshvardhan handed her one of the tall glasses full of brown liquid with ice cubes and fresh mint leaves floating in it, before sitting down on an adjacent sofa.

Dayanita sipped from her glass, her eyes closed as she savoured the taste. "Mmm… this is just amazing, even better than what we had at the bar," she declared.

Her face was a study in sensuality. Harshvardhan forgot to drink as he placed his glass on the centre table and simply gazed at her in amazement. Her eyes were shut, the long and curling lashes resting like fans on her cheeks while she opened her luscious lips slightly to take another sip. He crossed his legs to hide his body's reaction, unable to take his eyes off her.

"Would you like to have something to munch now?"

She opened her eyes that reminded him of melting chocolate unlike the fiery volcano that had tried to burn him down during their first few meetings. "Not really. I'm good." She didn't want to spoil her appetite for dinner.

"Shall I ask them to bring dinner?" he asked, "unless you want to have another drink."

"No, this is enough. I'm more than ready for dinner actually. I'm famished," she said, rubbing her hand against her stomach.

Harshvardhan's eyes were drawn to her flat stomach and he felt a sudden urge to touch her. Bringing his eyelids down to hide the expression in his eyes, he picked up the phone to place the order, without bothering to consult her. The hotel kitchen was under renovation and there was only a limited fare on offer. He asked them to put together a platter of a bit of everything and bring it to his suite.

Dayanita stepped out of the French windows to look at the garden, breathing deeply of the fragrance of oranges. This area was facing the opposite side as the bar's terrace. She was feeling lightheaded after drinking three rounds of the highly potent iced tea, Harshvardhan's nearness only adding to the feeling. While the gentle breeze from the garden was soothing, it didn't go a long way to clearing her head.

She had noticed the glances he had been stealing at her. Not the ones when they were chatting. These were the secret glances he kept giving her, as he checked her out from various angles, his desire obvious. Each time his charcoal gaze fell on her breasts, she could feel them throb, the nipples tightening. It was a good thing that she had chosen to wear a bustier underneath her silk sheath dress or her body would have betrayed her aroused state to him.

"Nita." Harshvardhan had stepped out too and stood directly behind her, placing his hands on the railing right next to hers on both sides, his body heat consuming her even though they were not touching.

Unable to stop herself, Dayanita leaned back on his wide chest with a sigh, her head bowed as if in surrender.

"Nita…" He lifted his hands off the railing to wrap his arms around her slender waist, gathering her close to his body, bending his head to place his chin in the crook of her shoulder. The deep breaths he took, hoping to control his libido, only seemed to arouse him all the more as he drew in her scent with every intake. Feeling her pulse flutter against his cheek, he turned his head slightly to press his lips to the side of her neck, stroking it gently back and forth with his damp tongue.

Dayanita moaned, lifting her hands to hold his arms that were crossed over her body, tilting her head to give him better access, thrilled to feel the rasp of his tongue against her fast-beating pulse.

Harshvardhan pressed soft kisses from her neck down the slope of her shoulder, his teeth joining his tongue as he took small nips of her silky skin, careful not to mark the golden smoothness.

Her head fell back on his shoulder as Dayanita gave herself up to his caresses, her small teeth biting into her lower lip, feeling as if her whole body was on fire.

Harshvardhan turned her around in his arms, his hands at her back now, drawing her close to his aroused body, his lips on her hot cheek as he traced a path towards the corner of her mouth.

"Nita?"

"Kiss me, Harsh. Now." Dayanita ordered, craving to feel his lips on hers. Having never been kissed before, she didn't really know what to expect. Only that Harshvardhan's lips on her neck and shoulder set her on fire for more of his touch and kisses.

"With pleasure," he said, pressing his lips to her soft mouth. He took her lower lip between his teeth and nibbled gently, making her melt in his arms.

Dayanita threw her arms on his shoulders and locked her hands behind his neck, going on tiptoe to give him better access.

When he raised his head to look down at her, she lifted her face to nibble his sensuous lower lip, making mewling noises at the back of her throat as she ran her tongue over his lip several times, loving the taste.

"You taste good," she declared, looking into his eyes.

His eyes glowed with both delight and amusement as he looked down at her, her lips red with all the attention he had been paying them, the pink lipstick having disappeared completely. He pressed his forehead to hers. "We haven't even kissed properly yet."

"We haven't?" She fluttered her eyelashes at him, refusing to admit to the shyness she felt.

Harshvardhan didn't miss the innocence on her face. While Princess Dayanita might pretend to be a woman of the world, it was obvious to him that she had never even been properly kissed.

When he shook his head, she said, "So what are we waiting for?" before pulling his head down to hers.

Only too happy to oblige, Harshvardhan pressed his mouth to hers, his tongue seeking entry into the pleasures within.

Dayanita parted her lips only to go up in flames the moment she felt his rough tongue slide inside as he slowly explored every nook and corner in a leisurely fashion. Oh my God! He was simply fantastic.

It was the ringing of the doorbell that finally brought them apart, both of them breathless with the needs raging through them.

"That must be our dinner."

Dayanita nodded, her eyes on his.

"Saved by the bell," he said, walking towards the door.

"So, who wants to be saved?" she muttered, scowling.

Harshvardhan burst out laughing, opening the door to let the waiter in. The latter strolled in with a trolley full of small dishes.

"Why don't you leave the trolley here? We'll help ourselves." Dayanita spoke to the waiter. She felt impatient, hating the interruption. But then, Harshvardhan was probably hungry for food and must want his dinner.

"Come here." Harshvardhan opened his arms wide the moment the waiter shut the door behind him.

She didn't need a second invitation before Dayanita leaped into his waiting arms.

He bent down to give her a quick kiss before removing his arms from around her, even as she protested loudly. "Easy, babe. Let's have some dinner first. You were hungry, remember?" Though there was a teasing smile in his voice and face, Harshvardhan couldn't hide the craving on his face which was only for her.

Dayanita pouted, nodding slowly, her mind not at all on food.

"Come." Harshvardhan drew the trolley close to the sofa, sitting on it before pulling her down on his lap. To Dayanita's surprise and delight, he fed her with his own hand, popping titbits into her mouth, seeming to gain pleasure from simply watching her eat.

"Let me." She fed him in turn, groaning when he took a bite of her fingers along with the *hummus* and *grilled naan*. "Harsh…"

He pulled an earring off her earlobe, taking a bite of the tender flesh. "Have you had enough?"

"Hmm… here, you have had almost nothing." She fed him some more of the *spaghetti*.

After taking a mouthful of *spaghetti*, he took the fork from her hands and threw it on the trolley where it fell with a clatter. Munching and swallowing the food in a hurry, he said, "I'm not hungry for food. Will you have some *chocolate soufflé*?"

She shook her head slowly, a great daring in her eyes. "I wanna have you for dessert."

Harshvardhan jumped off the sofa with a groan, lifting her up in his arms to carry her to the bedroom. He paused for a moment on reaching the bed. "Are you sure?"

"Never more so," she declared, burying her face in his shoulder.

Harshvardhan carried Dayanita as if she weighed nothing before gently letting go off her near the king-sized bed. He lifted a hand to pull the two silver clips that held her hair in a top knot and watched in amazement as the luxurious dark brown locks tumbled down her shoulders and fell to her waist.

Splaying his fingers through her hair, he lifted her face up to his, looking deeply into her eyes. "I want you to be sure, babe. Once we get in there, I will not be able to stop," he said, his voice hoarse with longing as he nodded towards the bed. He had to give her the chance to say 'no'. After all, he hadn't expected to come this far on a second date with the princess.

Dayanita looked up into his gaze that had gone smoky with passion and smiled. Going on tiptoe, she pressed her lips to his smooth cheek, her arms going around his lean waist. "Yes," she spoke into his ear with all the eagerness she could muster.

With a whoop of triumph, he lifted her up and laid her down in the middle of the bed, joining her there. Holding both her hands in his, he pressed them down on the bed, bending his head to kiss her forehead. With his lips he traced the shape of her eyebrows before dropping soft kisses on her closed eyelids, smiling when he felt her eyelashes flutter against his lips. When he pressed his mouth to her right cheek, Dayanita turned her head to bite his lower lip, demanding that he kiss her properly.

Laughing, Harshvardhan let go of her hands to gather her close to his body, kissing her long and hard, pleasuring her thoroughly with his lips, teeth and tongue. It was a while before they came up for air, Dayanita burying her face in his shoulder, scowling when she couldn't reach his skin.

"Aren't you wearing too many clothes?" she grumbled, moving away to glare at him.

He laughed again. "So, would you like to help me take them off?"

Her eyes glowed with excitement as Dayanita sat up on the bed, an intense look on her face when she pulled at the knot of his tie, her hands trembling slightly when she pulled the pearl buttons from the buttonholes.

Harshvardhan swiftly shrugged out of his suit jacket even as Dayanita pulled back the flaps of his white shirt, eyeing his magnificent chest with awe on her face, her mouth open as she stared at him.

Having two brothers, she wasn't really unfamiliar with naked chests. But then Indrajeet and Rajvardhan were her brothers and didn't really count. Prince Harshvardhan Singh Gaekwad was something else altogether. With wide shoulders tapering into a lean waist, his V-shaped body was a sight to behold.

Harshvardhan sat in front of her, gritting his teeth, his jaw hard as he fought for control while he watched the myriad expressions running across Dayanita's face as she studied him.

She lifted a hand as if to touch him, before withdrawing it as an unexpected shyness overwhelmed her. She wasn't given to touching people easily, another legacy given to her by her grandmother. Will she like touching him? And what if he didn't care for her hands on his body? Her whole body thrummed with unfamiliar sensations as she continued to stare at his spectacular chest, holding her hands into tight fists, fearing that she might lose control over them.

Seeing her hesitation, Harshvardhan took a small fist in his hand and gently opened it before placing her hand on his chest. "Go on," he said softly, "I'm all yours to explore."

Her eyes going wide due to the tingling feeling in her palm, Dayanita ran a hand over his hair-roughened chest, getting totally absorbed by the tactile sensation. She felt like a kid in a toyshop as she went on her knees before him, her other hand joining the first as she explored him from shoulder to waist. She paused when her hand encountered a flat male nipple, before tracing it over, round and round with her thumb, fascinated to see it tightening into a sharp nub.

"Nita…" Harshvardhan groaned, pulling her into his arms. "I want to touch you too."

She lifted her startled gaze up to his, colour flaring in her cheeks. "Er… I…"

Harshvardhan reached out to run his hands from her bare shoulders down her arms. He removed her armlet and placed it on a side table. Soon, her necklace and a single earring joining it. He remembered dropping the first earring somewhere near the sofa in the living room. "How do I get your dress off?" He couldn't find a hook or a zip for it when he ran his fingers over the edge.

Dayanita lifted her left arm high and turned that side towards him to show him the tiny hook and zip that held the garment in place.

With a soft sigh, Harshvardhan unhooked the dress, pulling the zip down, peeling the figure-hugging pink silk from her body, on the verge of drooling when his eyes fell on the lacy bustier of a darker pink shade that held her lush breasts in its hold.

Dayanita got off from the bed to shimmy out of her dress before sitting down again on the edge. As she bent down to take off her heels, Harshvardhan laid a hand on her arm. "Let me."

He got down from the bed and went on his knees in front of her, his hands at her slender ankle as he removed the buckle that held her shoe in place. Removing the shoes one by one, he held a narrow foot in his large hands, stroking it firmly.

"Aah!" Dayanita moaned as her foot revelled in his strokes. He seemed to know the exact spots to touch, making her simply melt as she looked down at his dark head that was on a level with her thighs.

Harshvardhan lifted her right foot up to take a small bite of her big toe, making her groan again. "Harsh…"

"You like it?" He lifted his face to look up at hers, a smile on his lips.

She nodded, "Oh yes!"

He took her left foot in his hands to give it the same attention. "You have beautiful feet."

Dayanita's heart galloped on hearing the compliment. No man had ever got close enough to say much to her, let alone words of admiration. Harshvardhan seemed to have crossed a number of barriers today. She placed her hands on his muscular shoulders, running them caressingly over the smooth skin.

Harshvardhan let go of her feet to place his big hands on her naked thighs, stroking them gently. Her skin was hot and silky to the touch, making him crave for more of her. He eyed her lace bustier, his gaze zeroing in on the darkened nipples that thrust sharply against the pink lace. Lifting a hand, he brushed a hard thumb over the tip of her left breast, making her moan ecstatically.

Without even aware of what she was doing, Dayanita placed her own hand over his and pressed it against her throbbing breast.

Emboldened, Harshvardhan lifted his other hand to her right breast, caressing both the mounds eagerly over the lace bustier, before he bent his head to press hot lips to the flushed curve above it.

Dayanita held his head in her hands, her fingers tingling as they ran through his silky hair, pulling him closer to her body, her breath coming in gasps as she felt his teeth nibbling the top of her breasts. "Harsh…"

He let go of her breasts as his hands sought the hook that held the bustier in place, unhooking it before pulling the garment off her body to throw it over his shoulder, his hands tracing their path back to her breasts, thrilled to hold their naked fullness in them.

She thrashed her legs restlessly, her hands clutching his head closer as she willed him to bring solace to the throbbing tips of her breasts.

Harshvardhan moved his face away, wanting to have an eyeful of her, his eyes glowing with need when he set them on her twin globes. They looked so perfect, plump and firm to the touch, the skin golden and ending in turgid pink tips that looked at him invitingly. "Nita, babe… you look magnificent," he said, bending down to trace the tip of his tongue over a sensitive tip, making her moan with need. While he stroked her left breast with his tongue, his left hand caressed her other breast, his thumb and forefinger tweaking the elongated nipple, revelling in the texture.

"Harsh, please…" Dayanita held on to his neck, thrusting her torso closer to him, trembling with need, before groaning long and loud when she felt his mouth close over her turgid nipple as he suckled her gently at first and then vigorously when he felt her eager response.

Wetness pooled between her thighs as Dayanita widened them, pulling him closer to her than ever, her hands running restlessly down his smooth back.

Harshvardhan let go of her nipple with reluctance, gently blowing on its dampness, watching it grow tighter before lifting his gaze up to hers. "Wanna more?" he asked, grinning at her eager face.

"Oh yes!" said Dayanita, turning to offer her right breast to him, watching in fascination as he took the tip in his mouth, his eyes never leaving hers as he suckled on it hungrily. "Oh yes," moaned Dayanita, "that feels so good." She took his hand to place it on her left breast that felt bereft.

His eyes smiling into hers, he squeezed the globe, his palm rubbing against the tip that was damp from his earlier ministrations.

"Harsh… how can I please you?" Dayanita asked him when he finally let go of her breasts to stand up.

"You already do, babe. Just give me a sec and let me get the rest of my clothes off." He removed his belt before taking his pants off.

Dayanita watched in amazement as his strong and muscular legs came into view inch by inch. "Oh my God! You look fantastic," she gasped, admiration in her brown gaze.

His shaft twitched painfully in response to her words as Harshvardhan pulled her up from where she was sitting on the bed and into his arms, groaning with satisfaction when her breasts came into close contact with his hard chest.

Dayanita pressed closer, loving the feel of his hair-roughened skin against her sensitised breasts, rubbing herself against his muscled chest like a small kitten, making him groan all the more.

With his left arm around her slim waist, Harshvardhan cupped her rounded bottom with his right hand, pulling the lower part of her body closer to his own, his legs splayed apart as he brought her feminine mound against his rock-hard shaft.

Dayanita's eyes went wide looking up into his, when she felt his hardness pressed against her body, before her heavy eyelids came down of their own volition. She thrust her eager body against his, loving the contrasting feel of his hardness against her softness.

He moved away to gently peel the last scrap of pink lace down her long and slender legs, his eyes avidly seeking the dark thatch that came into his view.

"Let me." Dayanita went down on her knees, holding the edge of his briefs between her thumbs and forefingers before dragging it down, her eyes going wider and wider as his manhood came into view. Her hands trembled before she stopped midway, staring at his magnificence with total absorption. This was the first time she had seen a man's body, so completely and gloriously naked. And that too at such close quarters. What would happen if she touched him? Putting thought to action, Dayanita lifted a hand to trace the tip of her index finger down the length of his shaft. She lifted her face up to look at him when he groaned in response while his manhood grew harder under her questing finger. "Does it hurt?" she asked, looking at the expression on his face.

Harshvardhan opened his eyes to look down at the woman in front of him, shaking his head. "No, it doesn't." Bending down to remove his briefs fully, he kicked them out of the way before pulling her up into his arms. "I need you, babe."

"So, take me," she said, smiling as she reached out to caress him with both her hands, fascinated by the silken sheath that seemed to hold a beast within as it twitched in her hands.

He lifted her once again to lay her down on the bed before lying down next to her. He began kissing her from the top of her head, down her face to her neck, pausing at all her erogenous zones whenever he felt her breath quicken as he brushed his tongue over each one of them. He nibbled her earlobes in turn, enjoying the sensation when she dragged her nails down his smooth back in response. "Little cat," he said, his tongue tracing the shape of an ear.

"I want to kiss you too," she declared, pushing him on the bed and sitting on his stomach.

He was sure she had no clue as to the effect she was having on him as he looked up at her glorious figure, her breasts thrust out proudly in front of her before she bent down to kiss her way over his face. He groaned long and hard when he felt her small teeth nip his earlobe a mite too enthusiastically, his manhood responding with alacrity.

"What? Did I hurt you?" she asked, her expression innocent as she looked down at him.

Harshvardhan shook his head. "Nope. Please go on. I'm loving it."

She bent down to run a tongue over a flat male nipple, before tracing the shape in circles. Raising her eyes to look at the blissful expression on his face, she nipped the tip, laughing softly when she saw him jerk his head, his eyes coming open even as his shaft twitched.

"You are going to be the death of me, babe," he groaned, pulling her up to give her a hard kiss before pushing her on the bed. "If I don't have you soon, I might just die." He ran a hand up from her knee to her thigh before dipping a forefinger into her core, finding it satisfyingly wet. He caressed her with his finger, drawing her right leg around his waist, even as he latched on to a breast tip with his mouth, suckling her hard. When she was all wet and ready, he took a condom from the table next to the bed and sheathed himself before rising above her.

Taking her mouth in a deep kiss, he pushed his shaft gently into her vagina, moving little by little until he hit the barrier. "Sorry to hurt you, babe," he groaned, pushing harder before settling deep within her. He paused, waiting for her to adjust to him, gritting his teeth in control.

Dayanita threw her left leg also around his waist, locking her ankles around him, her nails digging into his back, egging him on. The pain that had hit her disappeared almost immediately before her body begged for the pleasure that seemed to be just out of reach. "Harsh…" she whispered, pressing her lips to his ear as she traced the shape with her tongue.

He pulled out of her to plunge in again, both of them groaning as one as they were caught in the rhythm that was as old as time, working their way to an explosive climax. Stars exploded behind Dayanita's eyelids as she felt the tremors that rose to a crescendo before she felt as if her body had been catapulted into a freefall. It was a long time before she came down to earth.

Exhausted and completely satisfied, Harshvardhan rested beside her, holding her trembling body close to his. "Are you okay, babe?" he asked, kissing her softly on her cheek.

Dayanita blushed as she opened slumberous brown eyes to look into his smoky grey gaze, saying, "Never been better."

He laughed, his expression turning smug as he pulled the comforter over both of them. The real princess was simply adorable.

Spooned against his hard body, she fell into a deep sleep for the first time since he came into her life five days ago.

Raksha Nanda glared at Pradeep Miraskar, the head of the talent agency she had hired to find her work. "Do you realise that my career has taken a nosedive in the past six months? Why the hell am I paying you so much?"

Raksha had been one of the ten finalists in the Miss India contest five years ago. She had been a much sought-after supermodel since then, gracing the covers of fashion magazines and doing ramp walks at almost all the famous fashion shows in India. But her desperation to become an actress had brought down her market value.

What Raksha refused to accept was that while she was an excellent model, what with her lovely face and perfect figure, she could not act to save her life. And then there was her snooty attitude.

Pradeep Miraskar's talent agency was more than a decade old. And he and his team were really good at their work. The company had started off representing models and later branched into representing wannabe actors. Pradeep Miraskar was slowly and surely making a good name for himself as most of his clients got regular assignments. And there was one huge feather in his cap. Harshvardhan Singh Gaekwad had been launched into Bollywood via Pradeep's agency and had gone on to become the star that he was today.

He could say that taking on Raksha Nanda's contract had been the worst decision of his agency. When he had signed her on two years ago, it had been as a model. She had suddenly got it into her head that she wanted to be an actress. Pradeep had recommended that she join the acting course that his agency conducted for a period of three months. She had stood last in the class of thirty and passed only because they didn't fail anyone in the course.

From the day Raksha had hired his agency, she had insisted on dealing only with him. "I will talk only to the owner and none else," she had told categorically when the best of his team had spoken to her.

Well, she was a client and a top model at that. Before signing a contract with her, he had heard from the market that she had broken her earlier contract with the other agency she had been working with before she became a Miss India finalist. What Pradeep didn't know was that the agency had put their foot down and refused to renew her contract as they didn't want to work with the temperamental model any longer.

"Well, Raksha, it's like this." Pradeep decided that it was time to be frank with her. "You have been refusing modelling assignments without even consulting me. I…"

"That's my business. Your job is to get me roles in films," she yelled, an ugly expression on her face.

He shrugged, a stony expression on his. "You're still young and have a great body. I suggest that you don't quit modelling. It'd definitely bring you a lot of money." It was not for him to point out that her skin was beginning to sag while a permanent scowl marred her smooth forehead nowadays. Well, make-up would go a long way in solving such issues, but it didn't make sense in her wasting time waiting for an acting role that seemed out of reach.

She got up to bend over his desk, her arms pressed down, her whole body aggressive. "I don't pay you to give me your suggestions, do you hear? I want you to get me acting roles, since like yesterday." She was shouting so loudly that most of the workers were looking up from their desk to stare in their direction in the open-plan office.

Pradeep refused to lose his cool, being quite familiar with the tantrums of creative artists. Well, not all, maybe. But he had met a few in his time. "I'll let you know when there's something suitable."

"I want to know *now*," she screamed, "You know a lot of people in the film industry. Call your friends and get me a role right now."

"Just get out, Raksha, now," his voice was a bit more than a whisper, in direct contrast to hers, "unless you want me to call the police."

Raksha's eyes breathed fire, a sheen of tears filming over them as she stood in front of him for a few more seconds before taking an about turn and leaving the office. She would get her lawyers to deal with the agency, she fumed as she walked out of the premises.

Her cell phone rang just as she got into her car. Seeing the agency's number flash on the screen, she took the call eagerly. What if Pradeep had changed his mind? She knew for a fact that he could help her if he really set his mind to it. He could work magic is what she believed. He had launched many fresh faces, both men and women. Look at Harshvardhan who had become an overnight star. Okay, the man had great looks. But then, so did she. How was she lesser than him in any way?

"Hello Pradeep," she said, deciding to forgive him.

"Hello ma'am, this is Kiran. I think I can help you."

"Fuck you, man. Who the fuck do you think you are…?"

"Listen, Raksha. You want a role in a Bollywood film and I can help you get one." Kiran's voice was insistent. Working for the talent agency, he ran his own side business of getting small time actresses and actors into the film industry through the back door. It all depended on how desperate they were to see themselves on the silver screen even if it was for a minuscule role.

She paused to think. The man sounded earnest. Why not meet him and find out what he had to say? "Okay, I'll give you five minutes of my time."

Kiran laughed. "That's more than enough, Raksha. When and where would you like to meet?"

"Now? I'm still outside your office. Do you want to join me in my car? We can go out for a coffee."

"I will see you in a minute," said Kiran, cutting the call.

Less than a minute later, he knocked on her car window. "Hello Raksha, I'm Kiran." He only gave her his first name.

She nodded, not bothering to shake the hand that he extended towards her. Once he had got into the front passenger seat, she turned to the driver and ordered, "Café Coffee Day *lekhe chalo*." She sat back in her seat, not uttering another word until they reached the coffee shop.

Over many cups of coffee, Kiran explained to her about the ways and means one could get a role in films. It was a good thing that the place wasn't too crowded and they had a whole corner to themselves.

Raksha's face grew hotter and hotter as she boiled with rage. Finally, she raised a hand to stop him from saying anything more. "How dare you? How dare you insult me like this? Are you even aware that I'm a supermodel? Do you even know how much they pay me to walk the ramp, you bastard?"

Kiran gave her a sarcastic look, unfazed by her shouting. "If you are so in demand as a model, why don't you simply stick to it? I'll be off then and not waste your time anymore." He got up as if to leave.

"Sit down, you moron." She took a deep breath to calm down before talking to him. "So, are you saying that casting couch is common in our film industry?" She gave him a sly look.

He shrugged. "What's so surprising about that? I'm sure it's prevalent in all industries. Anything for a piece of flesh, especially if it's young."

She gave him a bitter look. She had had her set of love affairs, but it had always been consensual. This was ridiculous! But… but won't it be consensual if she agreed to it? It wasn't as if someone was going to rape her. She needed to please some director or producer and she would get a chance in a film. Once she got her foot inside, she planned to root herself right there in the middle of the industry. So, what was the big deal?

"Okay. But strictly no filming, get it? I won't be known as a porn star." She pinned him with her sharp gaze.

Kiran smiled, nodding his head vigorously, his mind already on the amount of cash he would receive for taking this super model into the producer's bed. Dhamu Sir was generous on that score.

"You don't worry about all that. You'll *pucca* get your role in this producer's upcoming film. And this is the right time. The casting has just begun."

Raksha got up to leave. "Tell me when," she told Kiran before leaving the coffee shop to get into her car.

"Raksha…"

When Kiran made as if to get into the car too, she waved him off. "I'm sure you can find your own way back to your office," she said arrogantly before telling the driver to take her home. Taking a deep breath, she shut her eyes to lean back against the leather upholstery. Just one night. What did she stand to lose? Definitely not her virginity.

I t was past eight in the morning when Harshvardhan opened his eyes, a wide smile on his face. What a night it had been!

Looking at the electronic clock near the bedhead, he sat up with a jerk. 8.45! He was always up latest by six in the morning, even after a long night whether at work or partying.

But, his smile turned into a grin, *last night had been special.* Harshvardhan was sure that he had found the love of his life. And she had been simply fantastic in bed. Being the innocent that she was, Dayanita had more than compensated for her lack of experience with her exuberance.

He turned to his side, reaching out beside him and was disappointed to find the bed empty. She was probably in the bathroom. He waited for a while and when she didn't materialise, he got up to explore, only to find that she wasn't there in his suite any more.

Had she gone for a walk in the garden? Harshvardhan drew on a pair of boxers in a hurry and rushed to the balcony to check out the garden. But the French windows were locked from inside. And her clutch wasn't lying where she had left it on the centre table in the living room. His gaze caught something gleaming from under the sofa and went and saw that it was the single earring that he had removed from her ear when they had been sitting on the sofa last evening.

But there was no other sign that she had been in his suite the earlier night. Dayanita had gone, left without telling him anything.

Harshvardhan shrugged as he returned to the bedroom. He will call her soon. Let her have some time to herself. The last time they had made love was at about five in the morning. He grinned, the look of a cat-that-had-got-its-cream on his face. She was probably resting. He could still taste her on his lips while he could smell her on the sheets.

Whistling tunelessly, Harshvardhan called housekeeping to clean up his suite before going into the bathroom to take a shower. It was Wednesday, and Dayanita must be going to college later. He decided to catch her in the evening.

Drying himself, he took his phone to send her a message, his face breaking into yet another smile when he noticed that there was a WhatsApp message from Real Princess as he had chosen to call her.

Thks fr awsm nght. No man cn cm a cls scnd. Bye

What the fuck! She had been a damn virgin when he took her last night. And despite that she had begged him to make love to her again and yet again. Not that he had complained, being only too ready to oblige. But what the hell did she mean by saying that no man could come a close second? Was she planning to experiment with other men? After all that they had experienced together last night?

Harshvardhan paled before colour rushed to his face, his temper blowing out of control as he threw his phone across the room where it hit the wall and broke into three pieces.

He didn't care. It looked like the real princess wasn't all that real but a fake after all. She didn't love him. Yes, they had met only a few times. But they had truly bonded last night. And which woman would give up her virginity, just like that, at the age of twenty-six, unless she at least liked the man?

It looked like Harshvardhan had been wrong in thinking that she had fallen for him just as he had fallen in love with her.

Was it a feather in her cap to let it be known that she had lost her virginity to a prince who was also a Bollywood star? He concluded that she didn't even like him and had probably been using him.

Harshvardhan hurried into the bathroom and threw up violently in the commode, feeling as if someone had ripped his heart out and torn it to pieces.

It took him exactly one hour to come to terms with his anguish. He dressed up and went to buy himself an iPhone, attached the SIM card to it before deleting and blocking Dayanita's number.

The real princess could go straight to hell for all he cared.

Dayanita did not feel like attending classes that day. When Andrea and Alia tried talking to her, wanting to know what had happened the earlier night, she replied to their questions with the briefest of answers.

"Come on, Nita. Tell us all. Harsh brought you expensive flowers and took you out for dinner. And you didn't get back home till morning." Alia fluttered her eyelashes at her friend, a mischievous smile on her face.

"You're so lucky, woman. So, what happened last night?" Andrea joined in the teasing.

The three of them had become close over the last eight months, spending a lot of time together, sharing secrets all the time.

"Nothing, guys." Dayanita refused to meet their eyes as she shook her head. Even she didn't know what was happening to her. How could she tell them anything?

Andrea's eyes widened mischievously. "You left home at seven last evening and returned at seven in the morning. Twelve hours with that gorgeous hunk and are you saying nothing happened? I refuse to believe."

Dayanita gave her friends a smile that did not reach her eyes, shaking her head.

"Don't tell me Prince Harshvardhan Singh Gaekwad is gay," Alia said, only half-joking.

Dayanita shook her head some more. If only he was! "I don't think so."

"Come on, Nita. You can't keep us in suspense like this. Go on, what happened?"

"If you guys don't mind, I want to be alone." Dayanita's voice was commanding.

Andrea and Alia stared at the woman they had befriended over the past months, surprise on their faces. They had never heard her speak to them in that tone before. Looking at each other askance, they gave a nod as one and left Dayanita's room, shutting the door a tad too hard behind them.

When her phone pinged, Dayanita decided to ignore it, thinking it must be from Harshvardhan, a huge sigh coming up from the depths of her being. He was too bloody handsome and a fantastic lover, gentle too. She would be the first person to admit to it.

But... but she simply could not let someone have so much power over her. And power is what Harshvardhan would wield, once he knew how deep her feelings ran.

Last evening was the second time she had gone on a date with him. How the hell had she let him make love to her, not just completely, but inviting him to repeat the experience a few more times?

The worst moment was when she had realised that she had fallen in love with him. It had been past six when she woke up, stretching her arms high above her head, her whole body one delicious ache. Turning to look at her lover of the earlier night, she smiled, reaching out to brush back the lock of hair that had fallen on his forehead as he slept on his front, his face turned towards her.

She carefully lifted his arm that was holding her close to his body before slipping out of the bed to go to the bathroom. She stared at herself in the mirror. It seemed as if her face had taken on a permanent rosy hue even as a small scowl gathered on her smooth forehead. She had had fantastic sex with the man. So, what? It was high time she gave up her virginity anyway. She was twenty-six, after all. Girls way younger than she were more experienced nowadays. And wasn't she lucky that she had a wonderful lover like Harshvardhan for her first?

Dayanita shook her head to herself, her scowl deepening as she glared at her own face in the mirror. Something didn't ring true in those thoughts. And why was that?

Well, Jake was handsome too and had been wanting to bed her from the moment they met, which had been more than eight months ago. He had made his intentions clear right from the beginning. She also knew that he had had many girlfriends before her. Why hadn't she taken him for her first lover then?

The colour drained out of her face, leaving it pale as a ghost, her eyes looking haunted now as Dayanita faced the truth. She had fallen in love with Harshvardhan, totally and irrefutably—with his handsome looks, his intelligence, his wit, his humour and especially the expression in those smoky grey eyes whenever they fell on her. His lovemaking had only managed to make her love him all the more. So much so that she felt that she was ready to worship the ground that he walked on.

NO!

No way was she, Dayanita Thakore, the princess of Udaipur, going to be any man's slave, even if he was himself a royal prince. She shook her head at her image in the mirror. Last night was over and done with. Today was a new day. Time to take herself off from his presence and get back to her own life.

And Dayanita dressed up in a hurry, shoving her jewellery into her clutch. There was only one earring. No matter! She needed to get away before he woke up.

And here she was, at home, all alone, but her own boss. She had made the right choice, hadn't she? Just to make sure that Harshvardhan stayed away from her, she sent him a WhatsApp message.

Thks fr awsm nght. No man cn cm a cls scnd. Bye

Men were such egotists. He wouldn't be able to tolerate the message, most definitely not. She couldn't think of a better way to keep him away from her. Dayanita was glad that she had her life back in her own control.

Then why the hell was she upset that she might never set eyes on Harshvardhan again?

11

"*D*i." Harshvardhan shook his sister awake, a hand on her shoulder.

"Good morning, Harsh." Princess Sitara Devi opened her eyes to smile at her little brother who wasn't all that little anymore.

"Good morning, *di*." He bent down to kiss her on her forehead. "I've brought you tea."

"Thanks," said Sitara, getting up to sit on the bed, taking the mug in her hand. "You do spoil me, Harsh."

He grinned. "You could do with some spoiling, *di*." He sat next to her on the bed, sipping from his own cup. It was barely six in the morning. Sitara was visiting her brother at his sea-facing bungalow in Bandra. She had no clue how to even boil water, let alone make tea. Harshvardhan lived all by himself, only having a servant to do the cleaning and washing. Whenever he ate at home, which was not very often, he cooked his own meals. "I'll be leaving in fifteen. I've made you some *kanda poha* for breakfast. I've also downloaded the Swiggy App on your cell phone. You can order lunch using that. There's also more tea in a flask, enough to last you till evening. Will you be okay?"

Sitara gave him an adoring look. "What will I do without you, Harsh?"

"I'm sure you'll manage very well, *di*," he said, giving her a hug, "and if I don't pick up your call, call on Mansi's cell. She'll get the message across to me." Mansi was Harshvardhan's assistant and an efficient one at that.

"You go on, Harsh. I don't think I'll trouble you. I have a meeting in the afternoon. Rituraj should be here by then to pick me up. I might be late getting back home. Will be in touch with you." Rituraj was her social secretary. That was only a title. He was the one who handled all the office work at their palace, managing the farms as well as assisting Sitara in her philanthropic work. He was flying down to Mumbai later in the morning and was going to accompany her to her meeting with a local NGO.

Just as Harshvardhan waved to her before leaving her room, Sitara stopped him. "Harsh, is something bothering you?" The two of them had only each other and were closer than any other brother-sister duo due to that, each one attuned to the moods of the other. She had noticed that her brother wasn't at his chirpiest best from the moment she had arrived the earlier night. His sunny smile didn't reach his eyes that seemed to withhold a deep sadness in them.

He stopped in his tracks, not turning to look at her. *"Nahi toh?"*

"Come on, Harsh. This is Sitara, your sister. What happened?" She got up to walk closer to him, placing a gentle hand on his shoulder.

Harshvardhan's big body shuddered, a heavy sigh bursting forth from within him even as he placed his hand over his sister's that was lying on his shoulder. "It's a long story, *di*."

"Let's talk tonight." It was a royal command. Sitara Devi was capable of playing the part of a princess to the hilt.

He nodded, looking down at her. "Done."

His pickup had already arrived to take him to the heliport in Juhu from where he was to travel by helicopter to Karjat where the shooting was taking place for his next movie.

On the twenty-minute flight to Karjat, he chatted with the few other people who were also from the film unit, working hard, without much success, on forgetting the one face that was at the top of his mind.

Dayanita! Will there be a time in his life when he wouldn't think of her every waking second? It had been two weeks since he had returned to Mumbai and he still couldn't push her away from the top of his mind. It was a good thing that he had been busy with prepping workshops and getting his body in shape for his new role. He had also grown a beard that the role seemed to demand. Today was the first day of shoot for his upcoming film, tentatively titled *Kuch na Kaho*.

The professional that he was, Harshvardhan pushed all lingering thoughts to the back of his mind, concentrating on giving his one hundred percent to the scene that was being shot.

At the end of the day, the director was completely satisfied with the rushes when he checked them on his laptop. Yashwant Mehra felt that there was a new depth to Harshvardhan's performance as he watched the actor on the screen. It was past nine in the evening when he declared, "Pack up," sending the film unit scrambling to follow his orders. Most of them were staying back in Karjat, in two bungalows that weren't far from the studio, while the heroine, Simi Kejriwal and a few other actors were staying at a local hotel, not keen to travel back and forth.

Harshvardhan returned to Mumbai alone in the helicopter, reaching his bungalow within half an hour of Sitara's return.

"Hey," Sitara greeted her brother with a wide smile on her face. "Want to have a drink?"

"Oh yes," said Harshvardhan, "just give me a few minutes. Will change and come." He returned, wearing a pair of cotton shorts and a vest before plopping down on a sofa.

Sitara brought him a glass of Scotch with lots of ice and topped with soda, carrying a glass of fresh lemonade for herself. "Here you go," she said, handing him his glass. "Cheers!"

"Cheers!" responded Harshvardhan, swallowing half his drink at one go. Placing the glass carefully on a side table, he looked at his sister who was seated on an adjacent sofa. She looked younger than him in loose three-fourth pants in linen and a matching t-shirt. Sitara was particular about wearing matching clothes even when casually dressed. Her face had been scrubbed clean making her look about twenty instead of the thirty-five years that she actually was.

He knew that it was best to tell her everything since she could be quite determined like that. Having had a difficult life with her ex-husband Raja Harischandra Gajanan before they got divorced, Sitara had grown a tough exterior. She was also of the opinion that trouble should be nipped in the bud. Now that she knew that something was troubling her brother, she would be determined to get to the bottom of the matter and would let nothing come in the way of her getting the truth out of him.

"So," she said, a dark and shapely eyebrow raised, "what ails you?"

Harshvardhan smiled at the quaint expression. "I met this girl in Los Angeles, Princess Dayanita Thakore. She's the princess of Udaipur, beautiful and charming to boot. Sparks flew from the moment we set eyes on each other. But..." he paused, his throat choking with emotion.

Sitara nodded, waiting for him to continue. Thakore of Udaipur probably meant that the princess was related to Prince Rajvardhan Thakore. The man had been in touch with her when he was putting together a case against Sitara's ex-husband. But right now, she didn't want to interrupt Harshvardhan while he narrated his sorry tale.

Harshvardhan sighed before continuing. "Suffice to say that the relationship cannot continue."

"You are in love with her," Sitara declared, not really needing him to confirm it in words.

Harshvardhan tilted his head in acknowledgement, not saying anything.

"So, what's the problem?"

"She doesn't love me."

Sitara looked into the deep well of misery in her brother's eyes that were so like her own, nodding slowly. "Does she love someone else?"

"I don't think so." He was sure of it since she had given herself to him wholeheartedly or so it had appeared to him at that time.

"Then what's stopping you from pursuing her? Making her fall in love with you?"

Another long sigh shuddered through him as he took one more sip of his Scotch. "It's a long story, *di.*"

"I'm all ears," said Sitara, leaning back against the sofa as she sipped from her own glass of lemonade, her long legs stretched out in front of her, crossed at the ankles.

He had been twelve when she had returned home from her broken marriage. She had become a second mother to him. While his parents had been heartbroken at their daughter's plight, Sitara had refused to break down under the strain. Instead of crying over her divorce, she had silently rejoiced having escaped from the demon who had been her husband. While Harshvardhan had been a preteen, he wasn't so young that he hadn't understood what had happened to her. He was all admiration for the way his sister had picked up the threads of her life and gone back to study, completing her graduation that she had given up midway to get married to Raja Harischandra Gajanan of Indore. Then, she had completed her post-graduation in Humanities and Social Science before setting up her philanthropies, giving herself a new purpose in life. The two of them had become closer over the years, especially after the death of their parents within a year of each other, always open about discussing things, with no secrets from each other.

Now, he decided to bare it all, telling her briefly about his first meeting with Dayanita until the time when he received that WhatsApp message from her: *Thks fr awsm nght. No man cn cm a cls scnd. Bye* that had broken his heart.

"Did you ask her about it?" asked Sitara, unfazed.

Harshvardhan shook his head. "Of course not. Why would I?" His temper rose yet again, as it did every time he recalled the moment he had seen the message.

Sitara looked at him with a smile. "I never took you for a fool, Harsh. But why the hell didn't you ask her about it? The words could have meant anything from her complimenting you in the only way she knew how or that she was simply teasing you. Or, maybe, just maybe, she had been using you. But unless you speak to her about it, how can you arrive at your own conclusion? She's a proud princess, obviously. And," Sitara shook her head at him, "you have blocked her number without giving her a chance to speak to you about it. That wasn't a smart thing to do, Harsh."

His eyes went wide on hearing his sister. Could she be right? Had he been hasty? Agreed that Dayanita was hot-headed. But she had been terrific in bed, giving as much as she took. And there was the fact that the real princess had been a virgin. Not just a virgin, but a twenty-six-year-old one at that. He shook his head now. "I don't know…"

"If you ask me, I think you should get in touch with her and find out what she meant by that message. And, by the way, your Dayanita is probably related to Prince Rajvardhan Thakore of Udaipur."

Harshvardhan gave Sitara a curious look, saying, "Rajvardhan is her brother."

Sitara beamed. "I've met Rajvardhan. You remember I mentioned that the Thakore prince had come to meet me about Harry? He wanted me to give evidence against my ex as Prince Rajvardhan was gathering material to have a warrant issued for his arrest." She sat up straight, keeping her empty glass away. "Just a thought. Why don't you go meet the guy? You might understand a little more about Dayanita."

"Hmm… I think you've an idea there. Let me think about it, *di*." He had a lot to digest as of now. To begin with, he needed to change his thought process on its head if he took his sister's advice. It seemed like he had probably judged Dayanita without hearing her side. His face brightened as he got up to give Sitara a hug. "You're the best, sis. I feel so much better now."

She grinned at him mischievously. "Aren't I now?!"

They laughed, chatting some more late into the night as they had a second round of drinks before calling it a day.

The next morning, Harshvardhan took Rajvardhan's phone number from Sitara. "Will you give us an intro?" he asked her.

"But of course. Tonight?"

"Perfect." Harshvardhan nodded before leaving for work, a pep in his step.

She hadn't expected to miss him, but she did, terribly. Dayanita stared at the professor in front of the class, a glassy look in her eyes as her thoughts were all around Harshvardhan. Finally, it seemed that she had got what she had wanted all along—for the prince to disappear from her life. She had sent that message to push him away from her, scared of her own deep feelings towards him. Now why was she unhappy that he had left her alone?

It was over a month since they had texted or spoken to each other. And she was too proud to get in touch with him. A deep sigh shuddered through her slender body as she recalled his smile, the heat of desire that leaped from his smoky grey gaze and most of all, his touch that made her sizzle.

How the hell could someone become so addicted after spending just the one night in her lover's arms?

She straightened her shoulders, a determined look on her face. It was best to forget him and get on with her life.

Over time, she found how empty those words were.

It was past nine in the night when Kiran went to Raksha's house. He had called her earlier in the day to instruct her to be ready to go meet Dhamu Sir, the producer. Nobody knew the man's real name as the whole industry called him Dhamu Sir.

A servant opened the door to Raksha's plush apartment in a western suburb of Mumbai, pointing to a sofa before saying, "Madam will come in five minutes."

Kiran made himself comfortable as he settled back against the luxurious sofa loaded with plump cushions. His ran his eyes around the living room, taking in the furniture and fittings before zeroing in on the many awards that graced a cabinet fitted with glass doors. Raksha Nanda had been—still could be—a supermodel. But it looked like she was ready to stoop to any level to become a part of Bollywood. He mentally shrugged his shoulders. It was because of the likes of her that people like him thrived. Tonight, he planned to find out how far she was ready to go.

He looked up when she walked in, dressed in a calf-length black dress that clung to her curves, leaving very little to the imagination. "Raksha…" he smiled, getting up to walk towards her. Throwing a familiar arm around her shoulders, he bent his head to kiss her on the mouth, just a chaste kiss. When she didn't object to that, he lifted a hand and squeezed her breast, his eyes looking into hers.

She slapped his hand away, snarling, "You pimp, you'd better stay within your character."

A man had to try, right? He lifted both his hands up in a gesture of apology. "You're right, Raksha. Can I have a drink? If you have Johnny Walker, that is."

"I don't want to be late." If he thought she was going to entertain him, he was thoroughly mistaken.

Kiran didn't miss the turbulence in the dark eyes that looked at him. What could he do? It was her choice to spend the night with the film producer. He was only here to help her out. "Are you ready to leave?"

"As ready as I will ever be," she muttered, nodding to him.

"*Chalo* then, let's go."

There was a full-scale party going on at Dhamu Sir's bungalow in Madh Island when they reached there. Most of the guests were drunk and lounging around in a haze of cigarette smoke, chatting and laughing loudly. A few corners were taken up by small groups of people. It took Raksha some time to realise that they were snorting cocaine. There were even a few syringes going around. Taking a deep breath, she gathered her courage in her hands and told herself that it was only one night of her life that she had to give. Once she had bagged a role in the producer's next project, she would get back to her life.

Kiran took her hand as he led her to the centre of the hall where Dhamu Sir was sitting on a single sofa in the middle while many people surrounded him, hanging on to his every word.

Raksha stared, her eyes wide as she took in the producer's girth. Built like an elephant, he was the fattest man she had ever set eyes on. How the hell was she going to survive the night? With a determined tilt to her chin, she waited for Kiran to introduce them. But the man had suddenly disappeared. Just as she was on the verge of getting a panic attack, he reappeared, carrying two glasses of champagne. "You might need this," he said, offering the glass in his right hand to her. She looked at him for a few seconds before taking the one in his left hand, lifting it up to say, "Cheers!"

"Smart girl!" declared Kiran before drinking the champagne at one go, snapping his fingers at a waiter before picking up another glass.

She wanted her wits about her tonight more than ever. So, Raksha took small sips from her glass.

The second there was a lull in the conversation, Kiran pounced. "Dhamu Sir, I'd like you to meet someone special. Raksha Nanda was one of the finalists of Miss India 2013 and is a supermodel today."

Dhamu Sir looked up at her with his swollen eyes that were red. His face was debauched, to put it mildly. "Hello Raksha darling, welcome to my home." He patted his thigh with a meaty hand before lifting it to beckon to her.

Raksha turned to stare at Kiran with blazing eyes, wondering if she had read the gesture right. Was the man inviting her to sit on his lap? And she had believed it would all be private.

Catching the desperation in her gaze, Kiran took pity on her. "Hehe, Dhamu Sir, Raksha has just landed in Mumbai all the way from America and is suffering from jet lag." He winked at the producer. "But she didn't want to miss your party, you see, that's why I brought her here directly from the airport. If you don't mind, she would like to rest for a while…"

Dhamu Sir laughed uproariously as if Kiran had cracked a hilarious joke. "Of course, of course, I understand. Why don't you take her up to the bedroom, Kiran? You know where it is."

Kiran nodded vigorously before taking Raksha by her arm to walk to the back of the hall and up the stairs.

Kiran kept up a casual chatter on their way up the stairs while Raksha gave him the silent treatment. Where the hell had she landed? They reached the first-floor corridor and he directed her to the left, pressing his hand on a door that opened to reveal a cavernous bedchamber.

Well, it had to be huge to fit that gigantic lump, didn't it? Raksha pressed a hand to her mouth to stop the mad giggle that was all set to burst forth. The enormous bed—it was even larger than the normal king-sized bed—must obviously have been custom built and was covered in jet black silk sheets with gold-covered cushions. And that wasn't all. There was a circular mirror on the ceiling. Ugh! While the bed took up a lot of space, the room still appeared vast with a couple of couches and tables. There were surprisingly no wardrobes. Well, the man probably had a dressing room. She wondered if he had a wife?

Putting her thoughts into words, she asked, "Is Dhamu Sir married?"

"His wife died a few years ago in an accident. He has been heartbroken since then," said Kiran, his face solemn. "You relax here, Raksha. Dhamu Sir will join you soon," he said, preparing to leave. He didn't want to miss the free drinks and food that were available in plenty. And there was also the gossip! Kiran always kept his ears open at such parties.

Raksha nodded without showing any expression on her face. She sat on a couch and waited for the next half an hour, checking out her Instagram and Facebook accounts from time to time while also playing games. The door opened sometime later and Dhamu Sir walked in.

She jumped up from her seat, her heart beating heavily as she watched the monstrosity waddle into the room, a wary expression in her eyes.

"Radha! Come here," he beckoned, his voice slurred.

Raksha didn't bother to correct him as she walked slowly towards him, taking one step at a time along with deep and fortifying breaths.

"Kiran tells me that you want to act in films," the producer said casually as he watched her with bleary eyes.

"That's right, Dhamu Sir."

"Then you have come to the right place. I can make you a star overnight," he declared, pulling her into his arms. "All you have to do is make me happy. Do you understand?"

"Yes, Dhamu Sir." Raksha's voice was choked as she whispered hoarsely, staring into his round face that was too close to comfort.

"Good girl. Now help me undress."

That night, Raksha learned that some things were way more difficult than acting—like undressing a man built like an elephant and worse yet, pleasing him in bed.

As long as she got her entry into the film industry!

13

"Hello, I'm Harshvardhan," he said, looking at the two men sitting at the table for four under a painting of Rani Padmini, wondering who Rajvardhan was. The other must be Indrajeet Thakore, he was sure. They looked too much like each other to be anything other than brothers. This was at the Padmini restaurant in The Lalit Laxmi Vilas Palace Hotel in Udaipur.

Both men stood up to shake Harshvardhan's hand in turn, openly studying him. "I'm Rajvardhan," said the taller of the two, "and this is Indrajeet, my older brother." The moment Indrajeet had got to know that the meeting was something to do with Dayanita, no one could keep him from tagging along.

Harshvardhan smiled, "It's a pleasure meeting you both."

They sat back to order beer, talking in general until they were served. "I met Dayanita in Los Angeles last month."

Both brothers sat up straight, all attention as they nodded in unison.

"I hope you guys don't mind my saying this, but the real princess definitely has an attitude."

Harshvardhan looked from one man to the other, checking their reaction to his comment. He had decided to be open with them since he knew that was the only way to get the answers he was seeking. He noticed the indulgent smile on Indrajeet's face while a small frown had gathered on Rajvardhan's forehead.

"What did you call her just now? The real princess?" Indrajeet guffawed as he took a handful of peanuts and popped one into his mouth.

Harshvardhan grinned in response. "She sure is one. Don't you think so?"

Rajvardhan was smiling too by now as he nodded. "You are right. So, did you get along?"

Harshvardhan shrugged. "Let me see, she almost beat me up the first few times we met." There was a reminiscent smile on his face as he continued to speak, almost seeming to have forgotten that he was talking to Dayanita's brothers.

"That bad?" Indrajeet shook his head, a grimace on his face, not at all surprised. For all her supposedly chasing after Ritvik Bansal, Dayanita could be prickly when she came into contact with men. She had probably been able to run after Ritvik only because he had kept his distance. Dayanita managed to push away any man who got within two feet distance of her.

Rajvardhan studied Harshvardhan's face keenly as he sipped from his bottle of beer. If the story had ended with them not getting along, the man wouldn't be here talking to Dayanita's brothers. He waited patiently for their guest to tell the full tale.

Harshvardhan shrugged, replying to Indrajeet, "In the beginning, it was. Then we went out a couple of times and got along pretty well. I…"

"Are you saying Dayanita went on a date with you, one on one?" Rajvardhan asked, an astonished look on his face.

Harshvardhan looked from one man to the other, noting the identical expressions of amazement. "Yeah, of course. I don't get it. What's so surprising about that? Isn't that how a guy and girl get to know each other?" His voice bordered on sarcastic.

Indrajeet smiled, liking the other man's attitude which wasn't any less than Dayanita's. Should he hope that his little sis had finally met her match? He spoke quietly now, answering Harshvardhan, "Chill, Prince Harshvardhan and I'll tell you why we are so surprised. Our little sis hasn't let a man get anywhere close to her. She's never had a boyfriend in all her adult life. Let me be frank with you," he said, giving his brother a quick look and seeing the agreement on Rajvardhan's face before continuing, "she's er… what one would call prickly. What?" he asked when he saw Harshvardhan's grin.

He was so relieved to hear from Dayanita's brother that she wasn't in the habit of letting any man near her. If that was the case, then she had been pulling his leg just as Sitara had suggested. Now he replied to Indrajeet, "Please call me Harsh. I don't want to stand on formality with my future brothers-in-law."

"Come again?" Rajvardhan stared at him, forgetting to sip from the bottle that he had lifted up to his mouth.

Harshvardhan laughed. "I'm going to marry your sister Dayanita."

"Are you sure we don't need to check your mental condition?" asked Rajvardhan, grinning at him even as he raised a hand in a high five.

Harshvardhan laughed again. "It's on par with Nita's. Since she's been let free into the big wide world, I suppose it can't be all that bad."

"In that case, we'll worry about the kids you bring forth into this world," said Indrajeet, getting up. "Welcome to the family, bro," he said, giving Harshvardhan a hug. "Has Nita agreed to wed you?"

Both Indrajeet and Rajvardhan had done a thorough background check on Prince Harshvardhan Singh Gaekwad before the lunch meeting. This was after Sitara Devi had called Rajvardhan to introduce her brother to him four days ago. And Harshvardhan had accepted his invitation to lunch in Udaipur today.

Harshvardhan shook his head, grinning. "She doesn't know it yet."

Rajvardhan burst out laughing, clapping a hand on Harshvardhan's back while Indrajeet looked on with a wide smile on his face.

After they placed their order for lunch, Indrajeet said, "Are you free this evening for dinner? I must invite you to our palace."

Harshvardhan nodded, "I'd love to meet the rest of your family. I heard you have a small baby. Aditya, right?"

The brothers looked at each other before turning to him as one. "That's right. Looks like Nita has told you all about us."

"Oh yes! She's very close to all of you, I suppose. Especially *Rajmata* Santhini Devi."

Indrajeet nodded even as Rajvardhan grimaced. But both were impressed, eager to inform their parents about the Prince of Baroda who was planning to wed Dayanita.

A feast was organised in Harshvardhan's honour and all members of the Thakore royal family introduced.

"I've watched all your films, Prince Harshvardhan, and I must say that I'm mighty impressed," said Chitrangada, Rajvardhan's wife.

"Thank you, Princess Chitrangada," he said, turning his head when he noticed another lady walk in with a small child in her arms. "Hello, is that Aditya?" he asked, smiling.

"Hello, Prince Harshvardhan. You are right. This is Aditya, the youngest member of our family and I'm Yashodhara, Indrajeet Thakore's wife."

Harshvardhan bowed his head in greeting before offering his index finger to the nine-month-old Aditya who held on to it firmly. Laughing, he said, "May I hold the little prince?"

"Sure," said Yashodhara, handing her son to their guest.

Harshvardhan took the baby in his arms and chatted with him, man-to-man as he made comical expressions, making Aditya chortle.

Ragini Devi was floating on air. Finally, her daughter had found someone perfectly suitable for her life partner. The prince was not only handsome, he was well mannered too. She watched him chat with her husband, Raja Gajendar Thakore, nodding his head as he listened patiently to the older man.

Harshvardhan got up from the sofa the moment he noticed *Rajmata* Santhini Devi enter the hall. He walked forward to greet the grand old lady with a smile on his face as he took her hand and pressed his lips to the back of it. "Glad to make your acquaintance, *Rajmata*."

Santhini Devi smiled at his bent head, impressed despite herself. To begin with, the Gaekwad prince was formally attired in a three-piece suit, looking truly like a modern royal. And his manners were impeccable, she decided as he offered his arm to her, guiding her to the sofa, waiting for her to sit down before sitting on the sofa adjacent to hers.

"I used to know your grandparents," said Santhini Devi, "and I must say that you look a lot like your grandpa."

Harshvardhan nodded in acknowledgement, a smile on his face when he said, "And now I know where Princess Dayanita gets her beauty from. She has your genes, *Rajmata*."

The old matriarch was floored.

It was almost midnight when Harshvardhan took his leave from Dayanita's family. "Please remember not to mention anything to Nita about my visit," he requested of her parents and the others.

They all nodded as one, fully aware of Dayanita's temper that tended to get out of control a mite too often. Harshvardhan pulled Rajvardhan aside to ask, "The *Rajmata*? Do you think she won't tattle to Nita?"

Rajvardhan grinned. "You don't worry. I'll deal with the old lady. You have enough on your plate dealing with my sis."

Harshvardhan laughed. "I plan to enjoy every moment of *dealing* with your sis," he said, a glint in his eyes as he stressed the word.

Rajvardhan looked at the other man, curiosity in his gaze. While Dayanita could drive any sane person up the wall, he couldn't help wondering what had brought on that particular expression in Harshvardhan's eyes. He curbed down the protective brother's instincts that rose within him. Both he and Indrajeet were in total agreement that Prince Harshvardhan Singh Gaekwad was a perfect match for their little sister.

Dayanita's friends stayed clear off her, sensing that all wasn't well with the Indian princess. The woman they had known since the beginning of their course seemed to have disappeared. This one was commanding, unfriendly and even rude at times. They weren't to know that Dayanita had kept her claws trimmed as per Indrajeet's advice. He had told her that that was the only way she could make friends. Once she got his point, it had been easy and she had enjoyed herself with the five of them.

But recently, Dayanita was totally frustrated. To begin with, she had done what she had done — sending him that message after spending the night with him—to keep Harshvardhan at arms' length. What she hadn't expected was for him to disappear from her life without a trace. Well, of course she could find him if she decided to go in search of him. But it wasn't what she wanted. She wanted him to chase after her and she would have loved to have had the opportunity to throw him out of it, yet again. But he hadn't given her the chance.

And there was this other thing. Physical frustration at its worst. If someone had told Dayanita even a couple of weeks back that there would come a time when she would find it a physical pain to miss someone's proximity, she would have laughed on their face. But the truth was that she missed Harshvardhan's kisses and his warmth. She missed his lovemaking as someone would miss a limb. How was that even possible? They had gone to bed for just one bloody night. And here she was recalling every moment of it. Damn it all! What the fuck had happened to her? Why couldn't she just put him out of her mind and get on with her life?

Then there was that idiot Jake! All this long he had only hinted at wanting to make love to her. But the night after she had made love with Harshvardhan, Jake had given her a lift home from an outing involving all six of them. They had reached home before the others. Jake had pushed his way into the living room and pulled her into his arms. "Nita, you look superhot today. I need to have you," he said, bending down to kiss her mouth, only to be shocked out of his wits when she pushed him bodily away.

"No, Jake."

"But why?" He watched her with frustration in his blue eyes. There was something different about her that night. A sudden light dawned on his face. "Did you make love with Harsh?" he asked, his voice hoarse with anger.

"It's none of your business, Jake." Dayanita had a mutinous look on her face, her brown eyes blazing as they looked into his.

"But Nita…" He walked closer to her, trying to pull her into his arms once again, only to have her move away adroitly. Jake realised that that's what she had always done, keep her distance from him. Only he had never read the signals correctly. Just because Dayanita had been friendly, it didn't mean that she wanted to make love with him. Damn! He had been wasting his time pursuing her. "You never wanted to go to bed with me, did you?"

She shook her head at him. "I'm not in the habit of jumping into bed with every man I come across." There was no apology in her voice. While she had been aware of Jake's interest in her, she had never reciprocated it nor had she ever given him the impression that she was interested in going to bed with him.

"I'm not just any man, Nita. We've known each other for nine months, damn it. I've made love to women that I have known for way lesser time."

Dayanita gave him a haughty look, a shapely eyebrow rising up. "With all your experience, it seems that you haven't learned to read a woman's body language, have you? Have I encouraged you in any way?"

Jake stared at her, shaking his head slowly. She was right. It was he who had been too sure of himself, confident that she wouldn't refuse him. What a waste of time! But then, Jake would never force his attention on a woman who didn't reciprocate his interest. To hell with Dayanita! There were other fish in the sea.

"Goodnight!" He left.

Dayanita rushed into her bedroom and shut the door, locking it. She didn't want her friends following her inside to sit around and gossip late into the night as they did on most days. Not today! She heaved a sigh as she removed her clothes before going into the bathroom to take a shower. Shutting her eyes, she stood under the hot water, recalling the earlier night in Harshvardhan's arms. Colour rushed to her face when she thought of the way she had demanded that he make love to her again and again. And he had been only too ready to oblige.

What did he have that Jake didn't? Or even so many other young men she had met? Even if she concluded that Jake was not an Indian, what about other eligible Indian men she had met during her life? Forget about wanting them to make love to her, she hadn't wanted them anywhere near her person. With Harshvardhan, she had just fallen into his arms after meeting him but a few times.

Rubbing a towel absentmindedly over her body, Dayanita stared sightlessly into the mirror as she brushed her hair, her mind on her lover of last night. She missed his strong and muscular arms around her. She missed having the freedom to touch him, running her fingers along the width of his chest, the crisp hair tingling her palms. She missed his lips trailing a heated path down the slope of her neck and his teeth nipping her plump breasts. Her nipples tightened painfully, making their presence felt as they craved his tongue over them.

Unable to bear it, Dayanita took her phone out from her bag to speed dial his number only to hear the message that his phone was not reachable. She quickly typed out a message on WhatsApp.

Hey, hw r u? call me

She waited through the whole night for his call or at least a reply, only to be thoroughly vexed. The message had not even been delivered to his phone in the morning when she woke up at eight after having slept for barely a couple of hours.

After waiting for three days and not knowing how to deal with the situation, Dayanita finally decided to go to The Beverly Hills Hotel and catch him there.

Walking into the reception, she said, "Could you call Prince Harshvardhan Singh Gaekwad in his suite? It's urgent."

The receptionist looked at her with a strange expression on his face. "The prince isn't staying with us any longer, ma'am."

Shocked beyond measure, Dayanita had to work hard at hiding her expression. "Could you tell me where he was headed to from here?"

"Sorry ma'am. That's confidential information."

It looked like Harshvardhan had dumped her after making love to her one whole night as if there was no tomorrow.

Hadn't he felt anything at all for her?

The next couple of months were the worst time of her life until she came to a decision. She was going to kill Harshvardhan with her bare hands the moment she landed in India.

With that thought in mind, Dayanita punched her pillows, buried her face in them and willed sleep to come.

14

Just as Princess Dayanita reached out a hand to open the door of the vanity van, someone stopped her. "You can't go in there, madam," said Anand, the security guard, politely. He could see that she was someone important from her regal bearing as well as the way she was dressed in a silk sari and heavy jewellery. But even with all that, no one got to disturb the movie star unless they had a prior appointment. And Anand would have known if that were the case.

"Tell Prince Harshvardhan that the Thakore princess is here to see him," she said, her voice commanding as she pinned the man with her sharp gaze.

Trembling by now, Anand offered her a chair. "Please be seated, madam*ji*. I'll inform the prince immediately." Saying that, he climbed into the van and knocked on the inside door. When he heard the actor's voice calling out to him to "come in", he opened the door to say, "Harshvardhan*ji*, a princess is here to see you," he said in a respectful tone. "She says that her name is Thakore."

Harshvardhan smiled at the guard. "Send her in." He turned around to nod to his makeup man who walked out right behind the guard.

The guard stood before Dayanita with a bowed head. "You may go inside now, madam*ji*."

She ignored him royally as she stepped into the van while he held the door open for her. Pushing the inner door without knocking, she stepped inside the air-conditioned comfort of a sitting room with a dressing table against one wall.

"Hello, real princess. We meet again," said Harshvardhan, getting up from the sofa he had been sitting on, standing tall in front of her, his head almost touching the ceiling of the van.

She drank in the sight of him like a starved woman, her eyes running from the top of his head rampant with curly hair—obviously having been set recently—down over his cheap white cotton *pyjama* and *kurta* to his feet thrust into rubber slippers. Her hands itched to touch his face covered by a thick fuzz.

"And no thanks to you," she said, her eyes blazing fierily, her hands clenched into tight fists as she exercised a tight control over herself. Otherwise, she might have simply thrown herself into his arms.

"Hmm..." he said, an amused glint in his grey eyes as he studied her from the top of her sleek head to the tips of her painted toes that peeped out from her open-toed sandals. Draped in a deep red sari of pure crepe, she was a sight for sore eyes, her face made up dramatically, her pouting lips painted the same shade of red. She wore a sleeveless blouse of gold that left her slender arms bare. It was with great difficulty that Harshvardhan kept his arms to himself, while desperately craving to hold her body close to his own before crushing her mouth under his. "Are you sure about that?"

She had the grace to blush as she looked into his piercing gaze, her eyelashes fluttering as it was an effort to continue looking into the smoky grey eyes. "Forget it. That's not what I came to see you about."

"Hmm…" he said again, his eyes lighting up with amusement as he saw the irritation flash on her face at his response. "Why don't you sit down and tell me all about it?" he invited, taking a chair even before she settled down. He had decided to be at his offensive best, the only way to make the real princess sit up and take notice. He crossed his legs, more to hide his body's reaction to her presence than any other reason, leaning back on the sofa.

That Dayanita was totally miffed was putting it mildly. She sat down with a thump and crossed her legs too, leaning back to glare at him. "I am pregnant," she declared, baldly.

Harshvardhan brought his eyelids down to hide the expression in his eyes as joy and desire burst forth within him on hearing her words. She must be pregnant with his baby. But then—he frowned—he had used a condom every time they made love. He concluded that she was lying, wondering what her game plan was. "Who's the father?" he asked, his voice neutral as he lifted his gaze to hers.

Dayanita jumped up from her chair, her eyes blazing brown fire. "How dare you? How dare you ask me such a question, you bastard? The child is yours, of course, who else's?"

"Maybe some other man's, the one whom you used to compare my lovemaking with?" he said, a raised eyebrow buried in the curls falling on his forehead, his voice cool even as his gaze settled on her flat stomach, curious to know if she was telling the truth.

"I hate you, Harsh, do you hear? I hate you," she yelled, jumping on him to hit her fists on his shoulders and chest.

"Stop it, you hellcat," he said, holding her fists in his large hands effortlessly. "Isn't it a good thing that this van is sound proof? Or the whole damn film unit would have heard you," he drawled, pulling her down on his lap.

She fought his hold, clawing the arms that held her down, lifting her face to bite his lips.

Laughing, Harshvardhan moved his head back, shaking it from left to right. "No, Nita. I have to report for the shoot in," he looked at the cheap watch on his wrist, "twenty minutes. Don't mess with my make-up."

"What do I care, you bastard?" she snarled, trying to pull her hands out of his and her body out of his arms.

"It's your child who will be born a bastard," he declared ruthlessly as he studied her face minutely.

Her face went red when she grasped the meaning of his words. Lifting her foot off the floor, she brought down her pointed heel on his foot. It was a good thing that Harshvardhan noticed her move, removing his leg out of the way in the nick of time or he would have been left to deal with a mangled foot.

"That's enough, Nita. You're getting out of hand now," he growled as he pulled her towards his chest.

She struggled in his arms, refusing to be drawn close to his body, more because she was worried that she might just snuggle into his chest and forget herself. "When did you ever have me in your hand for me to get out of it now?" she muttered, a deep frown on her face as she pushed back against the iron band of his arms.

Harshvardhan laughed despite himself. "You are right, real princess, as always." He pushed her off his lap suddenly and got up, walking a couple of steps away from her. Or he might not have been responsible for making love to her then and there.

She felt bereft as she watched him walk away from her. It looked like he didn't care for her after all and her trump card had failed. Squaring her shoulders and setting her back straight, she looked at his face with a determined expression in her brown gaze. "Are you willing to take responsibility for the child or not?"

"I have a condition. No, two actually, before I do that." He paused deliberately, knowing fully well that he was rattling her chain and having fun at her expense.

"You are in no position to lay down conditions," she snarled, her face turning redder than ever.

She was a sight to behold, the tempestuous Thakore princess. Harshvardhan enjoyed watching her though it was an effort to hold himself back from making love to her. "Are you sure? You are the vulnerable party here, real princess. It's you who can't lay conditions."

She gave him a sly look before speaking the dialogue she had planned in advance. "It's all fine for men. It's us women who are left to deal with the repercussions."

Harshvardhan shut his eyes in a hurry to hide the twinkle in them. *Abla naari* dialogue indeed! It was difficult not to laugh. "I agree that it's a man who must have impregnated you. It's just that I don't want to be landed with someone else's baby. You get me, right?"

"I'm telling you that it's your child, Harsh. How dare you doubt me?"

"Because I got a WhatsApp message that clearly meant that you were going to have sex with other guys?" He gave her a look from the corner of his eyes, his head tilted to one side as he studied her reaction.

Her own words had come back to bite her on her bum! Dayanita scowled. "You have to take my word for it."

"Science has proven that I don't," he declared, his arms crossed on his wide chest as he stood there leaning against the dressing table.

"What?" She placed her fisted hands on her hips, her stance aggressive as she gave him a challenging look.

"And that brings us back to my two conditions." He waited for her response, enjoying their conversation way more than he had expected. The real princess was something else when her temper was aroused. That she was a passionate woman was something he already knew. One thing he didn't understand though. Rajvardhan had promised to give him a heads up when Dayanita arrived in India. How come he hadn't kept his word?

Dayanita continued to scowl up at him. No, she wasn't going to give him the satisfaction of asking him what his conditions were. She was sure he would tell her anyway. She just glared at him, not saying anything.

"Since you must be dying to know, let me tell you," he said with a serious expression on his face, "I want to accompany you to a gynaecologist to test your pregnancy, and," he lifted a hand to stop her when she would have interrupted, "*if* he confirms it, I want a DNA test done to confirm paternity."

"Go to hell!" she said, turning away from him, thinking furiously about how to deal with the situation. To begin with, she wasn't pregnant. It had been a ploy to get in touch with Harshvardhan. And moreover, she wanted to shock him into taking notice of her, the lover he had ignored for over two months. She had taken a flight to Mumbai and had directly gone to Karjat to meet him. Even her family wasn't aware that she was in India. She had been confident that he would dance to her tunes once he was convinced that she was expecting his baby. But instead of that, Harshvardhan had called her bluff.

What had happened to the man who had made love to her long into the wee hours of one morning, worshipping her body?

She knew the answer. She had destroyed his feelings with that stupid message she had sent on the spur of the moment. It was time to retreat and come up with another game plan.

Making up her mind quickly, she opened the door to leave.

"Nita!"

She stopped, refusing to turn. Let him stew. He well deserved it.

"Be careful with those killer heels. You don't want to lose the baby, do you?"

Her temper blew out of control when she heard the sarcasm in his tone. Bending down to remove both her shoes, she lifted them up in the air before she flung them hard in the direction of the chair he had been sitting on, not stopping to watch them bounce off and fall to the floor, rushing down the steps of the van, annoyed even as his laughter followed her.

She didn't notice the news reporter speaking into his phone furiously even as a camera flashed. Dayanita was in an angry haze as she marched over to the car she had hired for the day, uncaring of her bare feet. She planned to reach Mumbai and take the first available flight to Udaipur. She was desperately in need of some pampering after all the insults that Harshvardhan had heaped on her head. Fuming with black temper, she ordered the driver to give her the bigger suitcase from the boot. Digging into it, she unearthed another pair of shoes and wore them before shutting the case with a bang. "Take me to Mumbai airport," she ordered the man, beyond furious.

It was not just the reporter and photographer who had noticed Princess Dayanita Thakore leave the vanity van. Raksha had been on her way to meet the actor before the shoot began. They were to share screen space that day and that was her excuse for meeting Harshvardhan in private.

Raksha looked at the car curiously, wondering who it was. That woman didn't look like any film actress that she knew. And she knew them all, if not personally, then definitely their faces, the way she devoured all film magazines.

Anand recognised Raksha as part of the film unit and didn't stop her when she entered the van. The inner door was open and Harshvardhan was picking up Dayanita's shoes and placing them in a corner when Raksha said, "Hi!"

He turned around to see her, smiling when he recognised her from the many ads that she had been a part of. He had been told that she had been given the role of an heiress in the film. He also knew that the role was minuscule. "Hello. Is the shoot about to start? I'm all set."

"In five minutes," she said huskily, studying him from the top of his head to the tips of his chappals. Despite the get up of an impoverished theatre director that he was rendering in the film, he was absolutely dishy. *Why didn't I get to sleep with him to land this role?* she thought bitterly before pushing all thoughts of Dhamu Sir from her mind. "I was thinking that with all your experience if you could give me some tips…?"

"Why not? Will show you the tricks on the sets," he agreed. "Why don't you go ahead? I need to finish something before going for the shoot." He had to get in touch with the real princess, or the rift between them might become way too wide to bridge.

She nodded to him before stepping down from the van.

Harshvardhan's attention was not on Raksha at all. His eyes glittered with excitement as he recalled the recent clash with the gorgeous Dayanita. The most important thing was that she had come looking for him. He almost laughed out loud when he remembered her expression just before she threw her shoes into the van. It was a wonder that the tempestuous real princess hadn't aimed them at his head.

He took out his phone to call the movie director. "Yashwant, listen, in fifteen? Sorry about the delay, but something unavoidable has come up."

"Chill, bro. Take your time." Yashwant replied immediately. Harshvardhan was a complete professional and was always on time, sometimes even arriving earlier by a few minutes. This was the first time the actor had asked for extra time.

"Thanks, Yashwant. Will see you soon. And *yaar*, will you please call Raksha to the sets, maybe urgently?"

Yashwant grimaced, saying, "Got you, bro. Will do."

"Bye, and thanks again."

Harshvardhan speed-dialled Dayanita's number. It rang and it rang much to his frustration before it stopped.

"Pick your phone, Nita," he growled before dialling once again. He had called her for the fifth time before she took the call.

"What now?" she snarled into her phone.

"Babe, where are you?"

"Stop calling me 'babe', she ordered.

"But you never minded before."

"That was before. I mind now."

"Okay! Where are you, sweetheart?"

"Harsh!" Her voice was a screech of protest now.

He moved his phone away from his ear, a grimace on his face. "Listen, Nita. Are you still in Karjat?"

"It's none of your business."

"I'm making it mine. Listen to me. I should finish shooting at six today. That's another nine hours. Why don't you come back and rest in my van? You'll find it more than comfortable. I'll take you back to Mumbai when I return by helicopter in the evening."

"And why should I listen to you?"

"Maybe because I love you? And don't want to live without you?"

"I don't believe you. You're lying." Dayanita couldn't stop the smile from splitting her face in two even as she pressed a hand to her chest to calm down her jumping heart. But she still continued to harass him as it gave her infinite pleasure.

"No, babe. I love you, absolutely, from the moment I set eyes on you." He was smiling too. He had his reason. The real princess hadn't cut his call but was still talking to him after hearing his declaration.

"Oh really! I don't believe in love at first sight," she said, leaning back against the car's upholstery, enjoying herself immensely.

"Then I'll just have to convince you, right? Why don't you come over here? Unless you are too scared to face me. Now, that, I will understand."

"Don't talk bullshit," she yelled, the smile disappearing from her face. She would show him, and how. "I'm coming over there, right now. As if I could ever be scared of you or anyone else for that matter. Huh! Driver, turn the car back to Karjat, to the film studio, now," she ordered the cab driver.

Harshvardhan laughed silently, his shoulders shaking with mirth. "I'll see you at lunch. Bye." He disconnected the call before walking out of the van, instructing Anand to let the princess back into the van and help her store her luggage as well. Whistling under his breath, he jogged on his way to the film set.

The car screeched to a halt when the driver applied the brakes before turning around to look at his passenger wondering if the woman was madder than even what he had believed before. "*Ji*, madam?" he asked, "Do you want me to take you back to the film studio in Karjat?"

"That's what I said," she replied haughtily, turning to look through her window. The surrounding hills appeared much greener now than they had a couple of minutes ago. In fact, the whole world seemed to be more beautiful now that Harshvardhan had declared his love for her.

Did that mean she was going to tell him what she felt for him? No way! She was going to make him stew just as he had made her fret when he had disappeared from her life.

Dayanita switched on some music on the hired car's music channel and hummed along with the songs during the time it took them to reach the studio.

Anand rushed over to help her with the luggage — one large suitcase and a smaller one. The rest of her things she had shipped directly to the Thakore palace in Udaipur. "Please come, madam*ji*," he said, opening the door to the vanity van with the key that Harshvardhan had entrusted him with.

With a half-smile on her face, Dayanita tipped him with a hundred-rupee-note, leaving him standing there with his jaw hanging wide open in surprise.

Stepping into the sitting room, the first thing she noticed were her red heels kept in a corner. She smiled before walking to the bedroom beyond. Equipped with a double-bed and a big-screen LED TV on the opposite wall, it was the height of luxury. Kicking off her shoes, Dayanita lay down on the bed, totally beat by now, what with the long flight from Los Angeles—even if she had travelled first class, the mad ride to Karjat directly from Mumbai airport and the adrenaline rush as she sparred with Harshvardhan. She felt totally drained as she immediately drifted off into a deep slumber.

Dayanita came awake as she felt herself being gathered close against a masculine chest. Opening her eyes in a slit, she saw Harshvardhan holding her in his arms. "Hi," she said, her voice husky with sleep as she slowly lifted her hands to lock them behind his neck.

"It's past six. Shall we leave?"

"Mmm… after you kiss me."

Laughing softly, Harshvardhan obliged her, letting her slide to the floor of the van before pulling her closer to him and placing his lips on hers.

With a soft sigh, Dayanita slid her tongue into his mouth to rub it against his. "You taste so good, Harsh. Missed you badly."

"Good," he said, with a slap to her bottom before crushing her mouth with his own.

Dayanita forgot her irritation as she revelled in his deep kisses and caresses, giving as good as she got.

He lifted his head to look down at her flushed face. "You look beautiful," he said, pressing his lips to her soft cheek.

Desire sparked in her brown eyes as she gazed up into his face. "No more handsome than you are," she said returning the compliment.

"Would you like to eat something? You slept through lunch."

Dayanita's stomach rumbled as if on cue, making them both laugh. "Oh yes, I'd love to eat something. Is there a washroom in this van?"

He nodded, letting her go to point a finger in the direction opposite to the bedroom door.

"I'll see you, then," she said, walking into the bathroom. Considering that it was built into a van, it was still extremely luxurious. On an impulse, Dayanita discarded her sari and the rest of her clothes to take a cold shower, coming fully awake finally. Towelling herself dry, she took the bathrobe hanging on a hook behind the door and wrapped it around her body, smiling as she guessed that it must belong to Harshvardhan.

He was waiting for her as she stepped out, his eyes running over her freshly scrubbed face. "Come along, I had ordered for some vada-pav and coffee and they just arrived." He took her hand to walk into the sitting room.

She was ravenously hungry as she bit into the vada-pav that was thickly layered with delicious chutneys. "This is so yum," she said, taking another bite. "Aren't you having any?"

"No, I'm good," he said, patting his stomach before pouring the coffee from the flask into two cups.

Dayanita relished her snack till the last bite, sipping her coffee in between. She got up once she was done and said, "I'll be ready in a jiffy."

He quirked a brow at her, his glance teasing. "Let's see. Do you need help?" he asked, tongue-in-cheek.

"You'll only get in my way," she said, making a face at him before walking into the bedroom and shutting the door firmly in his face.

Laughing, Harshvardhan gathered all the utensils on the tray they had been brought in, walked to the door of the van and handed them to Anand.

Returning to the sitting room, he was surprised that Dayanita, true to her word, had indeed got ready in a jiffy. She was dressed in a pair of denim shorts and a white tee, her long legs appearing sexy, her narrow feet tucked into a pair of suede espadrilles the same shade of dark blue as her shorts. Her hair was up in a ponytail, making him want to pull it free of the scrunchy that held it together.

"All packed?"

"Yep!" she said, pulling both her suitcases to the front.

"Let's go then." He took the bigger suitcase from her, careful not to touch her. He didn't want the pilot to wait any longer as they were already delayed.

"This is luxurious," said Dayanita, taking his hand to get into the helicopter. "You guys in Bollywood definitely lead a grand life."

Harshvardhan grinned as he pushed her gently into a seat before buckling the seatbelt around her. Sitting next to her, he held her hand through the short flight to Mumbai.

They walked to the car park to stop next to his car, Harshvardhan opening the boot to store her luggage in it.

Dayanita whistled as she took in the red Maserati, her eyes glowing with pleasure. "This looks so gorgeous, Harsh."

"You like it? Wanna drive?"

"You'd let me? In Mumbai's traffic?"

He shrugged. "Why not?"

"Yes!" She pumped her fist in the air, getting into the driver's seat on the left-hand side of the Italian car and adjusting it to suit her height before running a hand over the rich cream leather upholstery.

He sat next to her and directed her towards his home, smiling when she drove the car into the bungalow's compound with expertise.

Removing her seatbelt, she turned to throw her arms around his neck and kiss him enthusiastically on his cheek. "You are my hero."

"I am?" he said, grinning down at her glowing face before kissing her on her lips, running his hand over one bare thigh. "I need you, babe."

"What's stopping you from taking me?"

He gave a whoop of triumph before opening the door and getting out of the car. Jogging around the bonnet, he reached her side just as she stepped out. "Come along," he said, throwing an arm around her shoulders as he guided her into his home.

She stopped inside the living room, turning to put her arms around his waist, lifting her face for a kiss, her heart beating a wild tattoo. It felt so good to be in his arms again after all this long.

"Are you allowed to have sex?" Harshvardhan lifted his head to ask her, a small frown on his face.

"Huh? I don't understand. Why shouldn't I be allowed? What's to stop me?" Her scowl was heavier than his. Her body pulsated with need, her breasts straining against the constraint of her bra and here he was asking her silly questions.

He smiled slowly. "Did you see a gynaec?"

Wild colour swept over Dayanita's face as she pushed against his chest with both her hands, trying to get out of his hold, only he refused to let go.

"Nita?"

She turned around, facing the other way, unable to look into his smoky grey gaze.

"Is there a baby at all?" He bent down to nuzzle her ear as he spoke into it.

She shook her head from side to side, too choked to answer.

He laughed softly, nipping the earlobe, saying, "Thought so too." He turned her around to lift her up in his arms to carry her to the sofa before laying her down on it. He joined her there, drawing her leg around his waist as he kissed his way down her neck, pushing the hem of her t-shirt out of the way as he explored the skin of her abdomen before his fingers encountered the edge of her bra. "Help me, babe," he groaned, desperate need in his voice as he lifted her up to a sitting position, pulling her tee off over her head.

Dayanita reached over to her back to unhook her bra, her eyes on his as they reflected the desire that she felt.

Harshvardhan inserted his forefingers into the shoulder straps and pulled her bra down, his gaze on her luscious breasts as they tumbled out invitingly. "Nita..." he groaned again, reaching out to cup the twin mounds in his large hands, squeezing them gently before bending down to stroke a warm tongue over a turgid tip.

"Oh yes!" she moaned in response, her head tilted back while her hands held him closer to her torso. "That feels so good, Harsh, please don't stop."

"Never," he promised before closing his mouth over the nipple, suckling ravenously. "I've missed you, babe."

She bent down to press her cheek to the top of his head, her arms around his shoulders, shuddering as she felt the reaction to his caresses all the way in her womb. She reached out to unbutton his shirt, pushing it off his wide shoulders, her hands caressing his wide chest, rejoicing in the familiar texture. She made mewling noises in her throat as she bit his collar bone before rubbing her tongue over the area.

Harshvardhan removed his hands off her to swiftly pull the rest of his clothes off before joining her on the sofa, helping her out of her shorts and minuscule panties.

His mouth latched on to her right breast while his hand went lower to caress the mound of her femininity, gently parting the lips before exploring it with a finger.

"Oh yes! That feels so good, Harsh," said Dayanita, lifting her lower body up to press it against his probing hand, reaching with her own to caress his twitching shaft, guiding it towards her body.

"Wait, Nita." He rolled off her, down on to the carpet.

"No, Harsh, come back to me," she moaned, opening her arms wide.

"Just a sec, babe," said Harshvardhan, picking up his jeans to dig into its pockets and coming up with a foil packet. Tearing it across, he pulled out a condom before sheathing himself in it. He pulled her down on his body, holding her hips as he brought her down on his shaft, lifting his lower body from the floor to thrust deeply into her.

Dayanita stared at him, her eyes having gone wide at the sensations that bombarded her body before her eyelids came down, savouring the rippling sensations as she rode him, her hands clutching his arms for support even as he lifted his head to pleasure her breasts with his lips and tongue.

She moaned long and loud as a climax ripped through her even as she continued to ride him.

His hands clutching her bottom, Harshvardhan gave a final thrust before reaching his own climax, groaning long and hard.

Dayanita flopped on his chest, totally spent, her whole body tingling with pleasure as she buried her face in his chest.

"That was the best sex I've ever had, babe," said Harshvardhan, his voice breathless as he spoke in her ear.

"Oh yeah, it was even better than the other night," she said, unknowingly admitting to the fact that he was her only lover.

It was a long time before they stirred, making the effort to go up the stairs to his bedroom where they made love again before Harshvardhan fell deeply asleep in her arms.

Dayanita held his head close to her heart, running a gently caressing hand through his hair as she watched him sleep, a soft smile on her face. She was finally ready to admit to herself that she worshipped Prince Harshvardhan Singh Gaekwad with her body, mind and soul.

Raksha was thoroughly miffed when she saw the rushes of the scenes that had been shot that day. It felt as if she had been pushed to different corners while the others— not just Harshvardhan, who played the hero and Simi Kejriwal, the heroine— seemed to dominate on every scene.

And that bastard Harshvardhan, he had promised to help her. Well, he did tell her how to present herself, how to speak and how to face the camera. But none of that had helped. She had followed the director's instructions to the T. But had any of that helped her in anyway? Absolutely not.

What Raksha didn't realise was that while she had moved her hands and legs according to the director's instructions, she simply could not emote. Her face was stiff and even snooty as she continued to hold the confident look of the model that she was.

She wondered if she should get in touch with Kiran or maybe even Dhamu Sir. She had spent a whole night with the producer, not having enjoyed even a second of it. And all for what?

Should she maybe try to flatter Harshvardhan and get him to promote her? After all, she knew for a fact that she was beautiful and not all that old at only thirty-two. So, what if he was a few years younger than her? That was it! Tomorrow, she would get close to him. And she would only be too glad to sleep with the man—who was a royal prince to boot—if the need arose.

Having arrived at that decision, Raksha visibly calmed down. She would meet the hero the moment he arrived for the shoot tomorrow. She knew his schedule. While the rest of the cast, including the heroine, stayed back in Karjat, Harshvardhan travelled by nothing less than a chartered helicopter to and from Mumbai, every day. What she didn't know was that Harshvardhan owned the helicopter.

She turned around to punch her pillows before burying her face in them. Tomorrow morning, she planned to lie in wait for him in his van.

Harshvardhan was awake at five as usual. Dropping a kiss on the sleeping Dayanita's forehead, he left his bedroom to go switch on the coffee machine before going for a shower. Getting dressed, he poured himself a cup of coffee before going in search of his cell phone and found it lying on the living room floor near his discarded jeans.

There was a missed call from Rajvardhan and also a message. Opening the message, he saw that it was a screenshot of that morning's newspaper, a tabloid actually. The picture showed Dayanita walking away from his vanity van. The caption said:

NO LESS THAN A PRINCESS FOR THE BOLLYWOOD PRINCE?

Shit!

He called Rajvardhan who picked the phone immediately. "Hello Harsh. Do you know where Nita is?"

"She's here with me, bro. But…"

"Thank God!" Rajvardhan sank back on the sofa he had been sitting on. "None of us knew that she was back in India until we saw her picture in the news article."

Phew! That explained why Rajvardhan hadn't given him a heads up about her arrival.

"I wish I'd known Raj. I would have told you. Nita came to Karjat to meet me yesterday, directly from Mumbai airport." He suddenly exploded, "And I don't know how the hell the newspaper got hold of that picture and whatever crap they have posted in that article. I don't know what to say. I wish Nita's name had not been dragged into this. I'm sorry, Raj. Please pass my apologies to your parents and grandma. I…"

Rajvardhan laughed softly. "Chill, bro. It doesn't really matter. You know how the media is. And you are the biggest star today. If she's going to be your girlfriend, Nita had better get used to it. It's just that we were a mite worried that she was seen leaving your van when it was still daylight and wondered where she had disappeared to after that. The minx hasn't bothered to call us about her whereabouts. I saw the news and called her cell, but I suppose she's still sleeping."

Phew again! Wasn't it a good thing that the Thakore family seemed pretty chilled out?! "I've to leave in a few minutes to Karjat. I'm sure she'll call you when she wakes up. I'll catch you soon, Raj. Bye."

"Bye, Harsh, take care."

"Hey! Don't tell me you're leaving so early in the morning?" Dayanita stood leaning against the door of the bedroom, wearing his t-shirt that she had obviously picked up from his wardrobe.

"Good morning, babe," said Harshvardhan, walking forward to gather her in his arms before kissing her thoroughly. "Yeah, I need to leave. And listen, Raj called. Don't your…"

"Who Raj?" Dayanita blew the hair out of her eyes as she scowled up at him, even as she wrapped her left leg around his waist.

"Rajvardhan, your brother?"

"Do you know each other?" Her frown grew deeper as she brought her leg down to take a couple of steps away from him.

"Yep. Do you want to go with me to Karjat? I have to be at the heliport in twenty minutes," he said, looking at his watch, "or do you want to take rest?"

Rest? She seemed to have been doing nothing else since yesterday. Of course, she didn't want to rest! And how dare he just walk away after last night? Didn't he have anything to say to her? Agreed that he had told her that he loved her on the phone. But that was it. Nothing had been mentioned after that. "You go on, Harsh. I'll message you regarding my plans."

She didn't let on that she was on a slow fuse as anger built up within her.

Unaware of the undercurrents, he said, "You do that," as he walked forward to kiss her on her lips. Only she turned her face away at the last second and his lips landed on her cheek. Well, he would have to compensate for that later in the evening. "I'll see you at about seven, okay? Bye, Nita."

He left, closing the front door softly behind him.

In a fit of temper, Dayanita pulled his t-shirt off and threw it against the bedroom wall before walking into the bathroom. She got ready quickly and stuffed her discarded clothes into her suitcase before booking a cab to the airport. She would wait there to catch the first available flight to Udaipur. She noticed that there were two calls from home and a few more from both her brothers.

Settling into the cab, she called Rajvardhan. "Hello Raj."

"Hey sis. This is a surprise. When did you land in India?"

"Didn't Harsh tell you?" she asked, an undercurrent of anger in her voice.

"No, he didn't. I called him because of your picture that made the headlines in a tabloid. You…"

"What?" Why hadn't Harshvardhan mentioned anything to her regarding that? "What picture? Which newspaper?"

"I'll send you the screenshot. When's your flight?"

"At noon. I'll be home for lunch."

"Great. Jeet says he'll pick you up."

"That would be nice."

She disconnected the call. Should she message Harshvardhan that she was going to Udaipur? *Why should I?* And how come Rajvardhan and he knew each other? Tch! She should have asked her brother that. Before she could call him again, her phone pinged as she received the screenshot.

Opening it, she saw that it was her picture indeed, her red sari bright enough to catch the readers' eyes. She made a face at the headline before quickly reading the article. It was full of Harshvardhan's successful Bollywood career and one last line where the reporter wondered whether the Thakore princess was his latest arm-candy.

Sleaze! That's what it was and it didn't really bother Dayanita. She smiled to herself when she realised that that's how her family had got to know that she was in India.

The article was so brainless that it was no wonder that Harshvardhan hadn't mentioned it. But that still didn't mean that she had forgiven him. How could he just leave her the moment she had woken up?

Pouting, she got out of the cab and waited for the driver to load her luggage on to a trolley before walking into the domestic airport, not really surprised that no one recognised her from the picture in the article.

There was a different security guard on duty when Raksha got out of the hotel's car outside Harshvardhan's vanity van. He saluted her, wishing her, "Good morning, madam," when he recognised her as part of the filming crew.

"Good morning. I've a meeting with Harshvardhan at seven. I'm a bit early though. Has he come yet?" She knew only too well that he was yet to arrive.

"No, madam. Would you like to wait inside?" he asked, his gaze surreptitiously admiring her slim figure dressed in a white mini skirt and a red top that allowed a brief glimpse of her flat midriff.

"I'll do that," she said, waiting for him to open the door with a key before stepping into the van. The air-conditioner had already been switched on in anticipation of the film-star's arrival.

Perfect! She sat on a sofa, crossing her legs before taking out a cigarette and lighting up. She pulled in the smoke, totally relaxed for the first time since yesterday, confident that she could twist Harshvardhan around her little finger.

The door opened five minutes later to let Harshvardhan in. Raksha took deep breaths to calm down her over-excited heart, her eyes studying his face and tall figure. He was beyond handsome and he wasn't even wearing make-up. But… why was he scowling? Though even that suited him so well.

"Good morning, Harsh. I'm glad that you're here. I've been waiting for you…"

"But why? And have you been smoking here?" He was in no mood to be polite. He liked his privacy in the mornings. And he couldn't stand the smell of cigarettes.

She got up to walk towards him, laying a hand on his chest. "I shouldn't have?" she asked, her voice a sexy purr, her lips in a pout. "I'm so sorry."

He prised her hand off his chest before taking a step away. "Whatever you have to say will have to wait. I need to get into my costume and makeup or I'll be late for the shoot."

"Come on, Harsh. You know only too well that Yashwant wouldn't mind if you get a bit late. I…"

"That's only because I make it a point to always be on time," said Harshvardhan firmly. Yesterday had been the one rare occasion that he had been late, that too by ten minutes. And he had noticed something during the shooting, that Raksha couldn't act even if her life depended on it. His mind still on Dayanita and the mind-blowing sex they had had last night, he didn't want to interact with this clingy woman. And clingy she definitely was!

Raksha laughed flirtatiously, though she was fuming within. *Wasn't he a saint?! Only the halo was missing*, she thought angrily. It didn't even strike her that she was actually acting at that moment. But then, that was because she was frustrated and angry, feeling some real emotion, emotion that she couldn't portray openly.

She didn't know how to bring that kind of feeling to the fore when she was in front of the camera. She walked closer to press her body against his taut one, closing her eyes as she felt aroused by his proximity.

She placed a hand on his arm and pressed his biceps, revelling in the strength of his muscles. She was single and could definitely do with a boyfriend like him. He was not just handsome but also such an integral part of the film industry—just the kind of person she needed on her side.

"Harsh…" She raised her face to press her mouth to his.

Harshvardhan placed his hands on her shoulders to push her away, moving his face away at the same time. "Get out, Raksha, now. Before I do something that we both will regret."

"I wouldn't regret whatever you do to me. Can't you see how attracted I'm to you, Harsh?" she asked, running her hands down her own body from the shoulders down to her breasts and then to her flat stomach, a pout to her lips, confident of making him want her.

Disgusted, Harshvardhan stepped out of the van. Seeing his make-up man walking towards him, he said, "Good morning, Sarang. Come along in." Turning to the security guard he said softly, "Don't let that woman into my van, ever. You hear?"

The guard nodded slowly, saying, "*Ji saab*."

Harshvardhan lifted his hand to pat the guard's shoulder, making it clear that he had no hard feelings towards him. "Now go inside and tell her to leave."

Nodding, the guard went in and managed to persuade the reluctant Raksha to step down from the van.

I will show him, the snooty bastard! I'll show him never to wrongfoot me, she swore to herself, refusing to look in Harshvardhan's direction as she walked away.

Not saying another word, Harshvardhan went into the van, switched off the AC and opened the windows, running the exhaust fan to clear the atmosphere of the smell of cigarette smoke.

Sarang watched the film-star, not saying anything. He had been working with the hero since the beginning of the latter's film career and they got along well. He knew for a fact that Harshvardhan didn't like to talk much in the mornings when he was getting his make-up done. It was obvious that he was preparing for his scene during that time.

Just before they began, Harsh looked into his phone to check for a message from Dayanita and found none. There was one from Rajvardhan though.

Nita on hr wy bck hom

Thnx bro

He clicked the send button before putting his cell on silent mode, pushing all thoughts of the real princess to the back of his mind as he focussed on the scene to be shot that day. He would talk to her later in the evening.

Harshvardhan was not to know that the tempestuous Dayanita would have so royal a temper tantrum that she would refuse to speak to him.

17

I t felt wonderful to be back home, for good this time. Dayanita hugged her parents in turn, and her brothers, air-kissing her sisters-in-law. She touched Santhini Devi's feet before crushing the matriarch in a bear hug in a rare show of affection. Dayanita had missed her grandmother the most. Aditya was fast asleep in his crib and she had to wait until evening to interact with him.

After a leisurely lunch, Dayanita opened her bags and gave them all the gifts she had bought for them from the US of A before taking a big parcel and walking into her grandmother's room.

"Grandma," she called out before stepping in.

Rajmata Santhini Devi was sitting near the window, holding the morning's tabloid. "Red becomes you, Dayanita."

The younger woman went and sat down on the carpet at her favourite relative's feet, resting her chin on her folded hands that were placed on the matriarch's knee. "Doesn't it?" she grinned, her eyes shining mischievously. "I wish I'd known they were taking pictures. Would have posed better," she winked.

Santhini Devi patted her granddaughter's cheek, smiling. "So, how do you like Prince Harshvardhan?"

Dayanita shrugged even as her smile disappeared, all expression wiped off from her face. "I don't."

"Don't be silly, Dayanita. You wouldn't have spent the night with him if you didn't like him at all."

It was just like Grandma to get straight to the point. Colour ran up Dayanita's face as she looked into her grandmother's shrewd and wise gaze. She sniffed. "Well, I thought I liked him. But not anymore."

"What made you change your mind?"

"He doesn't love me, Grandma."

"Did he say so?" Santhini Devi smiled. The other day, when the Baroda prince had visited them, he had made his interest in Dayanita only too obvious.

"Say what?" Dayanita scowled at her grandmother. Why was the *Rajmata* so happy? What was there to be so cheerful about under the circumstances?

"That he doesn't love you?"

"Grandma! Why would he tell me that he doesn't love me?"

"Exactly. That's what I was wondering too. Then how did you arrive at the conclusion that he doesn't love you?"

"You have changed, Grandma." Dayanita studied the old and wrinkled face in front of her. Actually, Santhini Devi looked younger and happier than before. Less sarcastic too, though she was still a master at playing Devil's Advocate.

"That's not the answer to my question, Dayanita," said Santhini Devi, her tone sharp, even though her smile had become wider. She was a happier person indeed, what with the palace restored to its former beauty, being an active member of her favourite club and her grandsons making the Thakore royal name prouder than ever.

"Tch! Forget it Grandma. I just know that Harsh doesn't love me."

Santhini Devi shook her head. "You are mistaken, child."

"And how would you know?" Dayanita gave her grandmother a quizzical look. First, it was Rajvardhan. She still didn't know how her brother and Harshvardhan knew each other. Now, her grandmother seemed to know all about the man's feelings for her granddaughter. What was happening here that she did not know about?

"Didn't Harshvardhan tell you?"

"Tell me what?" She and Harshvardhan had barely had the time for a conversation since she arrived in India. She blushed fierily when she recalled what they had been busy with.

Santhini Devi didn't miss the colour on her granddaughter's cheeks. "Dayanita, listen to me. I know that you are a princess and need to be proud of your heritage and all that. But Harshvardhan is also from a royal family. You have always been prickly around men. But that doesn't seem to be the case here. You are twenty-six going on twenty-seven. This is the right time to think of marriage. I..."

"Grandma!" Dayanita's voice was a frustrated scream when she interrupted Santhini Devi. The fact that the matriarch didn't like being interrupted had been drummed into her grandchildren from a very young age. And it had been Dayanita who had always followed the rule. But… just now she didn't need this lecture. "How do I marry a guy who doesn't want to marry me?"

Her eyes shimmered with unshed tears of hurt and anger. She had been so excited when Harshvardhan had declared his love for her over the phone. And that's exactly the reason why she had rushed back to Karjat. But that was it. He had never mentioned the L word again, not once during the night. And here was her grandmother, presuming that Prince Harshvardhan was all set to marry her. What did the old matriarch know about modern relationships? He was a Bollywood star. For all she knew, he was into one-night stands.

Dayanita blinked. Well, she couldn't really say that she was a one-night stand in Harshvardhan's life. But… why the hell hadn't he said anything about loving her? This morning, he had just upped and left after giving her a kiss. She was all set to climb the walls in frustration by now.

Santhini Devi looked at her granddaughter's pinched face. She almost told her that the Prince of Baroda had visited them and as good as declared his intentions. But then, Rajvardhan had strictly warned her from saying anything. And that had been at Harshvardhan's request. While the old matriarch loved to poke her nose into all matters, she didn't want to throw a spanner in the path of love. She sighed deeply now, running a gentle hand over Dayanita's head. "I think you should give him a chance to declare himself."

"Huh!" Dayanita got up, saying "I'll see you later, Grandma," and left Santhini Devi's suite.

She went up to her room and shut the door before bolting it. She didn't want to be disturbed while she wallowed in self-pity.

What if Harshvardhan was interested in only having sex with her? Deep down, Dayanita knew that she was hot-tempered and threw tantrums at the drop of a hat. Even yesterday morning, she hadn't given it a thought before throwing her shoes at him. Well, not directly at him, but it was as good as doing that. She had been rude to him, many times. Why would he want to put up with all that?

She walked from one end of her room to the other, her hands locked tightly behind her back as she analysed herself, actually tearing herself into pieces. By the end of the long session of self-talk, she was filled with hatred towards herself.

If she couldn't love herself, how could she expect Harshvardhan to? Dayanita wasn't aware of the passing of time. Nor did she realise that her phone was lying downstairs on a table in the main hall. It was past seven when someone knocked on her door.

"Nita, are you awake?" Rajvardhan called. Seeing her wan face when she opened the door, he asked, "Is something wrong, Nita?"

She shook her head. "Nothing."

"Why haven't you picked up Harsh's calls? He's been trying to reach you since a long time."

"I don't want to talk with him." Not because she felt that he didn't love her. Now, Dayanita was clear that it wasn't possible for him to love someone like her.

"Why sis? Have you quarrelled with him?"

She shook her head again. "No."

"Then?"

She teared up again. "Tell me the truth, Raj. Am I truly a bitch?"

"What? Says who?" Rajvardhan bit his lip to stop himself from smiling. It seemed as if his sister had been doing a lot of soul searching.

"No one. It's just that I think... I feel that I'm exceptionally rude and have a terrible temper. It's not possible for anyone to love me." She looked up at him. Rajvardhan was a compulsive tease. How she wished that he wouldn't say something to pull her leg! Right now, Dayanita was in no state to take even light teasing.

"Nita." Rajvardhan walked forward to hug his sister. "You've been beating yourself up. I agree that you have a temper and can be rude." He lifted a hand when she would have protested. "But that doesn't make you a bad person. We all love you, your whole family. Why do you feel unloved suddenly?"

She buried her face in his shoulder and wept, refusing to say anything. Rajvardhan rubbed her back, letting her cry. She was obviously in no state to talk to Harshvardhan. Rajvardhan wondered if they had quarrelled with each other. But if that were the case, the other man was obviously ready to patch up, or he wouldn't have called Dayanita so many times.

Even then, he decided to have a chat with Harshvardhan. Rajvardhan didn't like his sister so upset. He waited for her to calm down before offering her a bottle of water that was on the nightstand. "Drink up," he said.

She gulped a few mouthfuls and kept the bottle away, giving him a pathetic look.

"Enough of moping, Nita. Have a wash and come down. Aditya's awake and it's time he met his aunt."

She nodded. "Okay."

"I'll see you then."

Rajvardhan dialled Harshvardhan's cell even as he stepped out of Dayanita's room. He quickly walked out to the open terrace on the side before talking into the phone. "Hey bro, is everything okay with you and Nita?"

"Why do you ask? Is something wrong?" Harshvardhan frowned as he chopped some veggies for his dinner.

"You tell me. Dayanita seems to be doing a lot of soul-searching. She seems to think that no one can love her because of the way she is. You know," Rajvardhan grimaced, wondering if he was doing the right thing in pointing out his sister's minuses to the man who was keen to marry her. But then, he couldn't keep quiet in the face of Dayanita's pain. "You know, she has a temper and all that…"

Harshvardhan laughed. "You had me worried, bro. I love Nita exactly the way she is. I wouldn't want her any other way. Do you get that? Is she upset? Should I come over? I can charter a flight and leave in an hour. I…"

It was Rajvardhan's turn to laugh. "I don't think there's a need for such desperate measures. And maybe a bit of soul-searching will do her good. And er… I have passed on the message that you called. I'm…"

"…not sure that she will call me back. That's okay," Harshvardhan laughed again, "let her be. I'll try to meet her on next Thursday when I have an off." It was another week away, but he really didn't have the time before that. "In case there's a need, will you call me?"

"But of course, Harsh. You have my word on that."

"Thanks, Raj. And bye."

Harshvardhan shook his head, a smile on his face. How his real princess loved drama! He called Sitara and chatted with her for a while.

"Harsh, can you do me a favour?"

"Of course, *di*. Need you ask?"

"There is this charity function on Saturday evening in Delhi. The chief guest has withdrawn at the last moment. Will you be able to come?"

"What time?"

"Seven."

"I'll be there." He would have to do a lot of adjustments, but he could never say 'no' to his sister.

"Thanks, little bro. Bless you," said Sitara. "I'm sure the organisers are going to be only too thrilled that the other guest cancelled at the last moment," she laughed.

"Hahaha!" They chatted some more before he disconnected, checking for missed calls and messages. It looked like the real princess was still upset. He decided to send her a message.

Hey babe I lv u. Cnt wt to c u

Though there were two ticks, they refused to change into blue through the night or even in the morning. Well, he could be patient like that. He would continue to woo his tempestuous girlfriend. Smiling, he sent her another text.

Whts up babe? U angry wth me?

Both sets of ticks turned blue simultaneously, but still there was no reply.

Ok dnt tlk. I stll lv u

He added a kiss emoji for good measure as he got ready to leave for work. The stubborn lady continued to maintain her silence.

When Raksha entered the foyer of the hotel where all the film crew were staying at in Karjat, she stopped at the metal stand holding that day's newspapers. She picked up the day's tabloid and carried it with her to her room. Not an avid reader, she still liked to keep track of the gossip column.

She was startled to see the picture of the woman in a red sari as she was leaving Harshvardhan's van. She sat up straight on her bed. She had seen this particular scene that had been caught on camera—the sari-clad woman walking away from the vanity van. She quickly read the article and smiled maliciously. So, that woman was a princess too. Princess Dayanita Thakore. What a horrendous name! She was sure the woman must be terribly ashamed of such an old-fashioned name.

And that bastard, Harshvardhan! It served him right to be featured in that sleazy article. Raksha rejoiced, thinking of his embarrassment. She was sure that chaos must have prevailed in both royal households after the news had hit the stands. Her smile turned into a grin as she got ready to go to sleep. She had been fuming all day at the treatment she had received at Harshvardhan's hands. Over and above that, she hadn't been involved in the day's shooting, having had to sit through the whole schedule, twiddling her thumbs.

Just as her eyes were shutting down in sleep, Raksha woke up with a start, sitting up straight on her bed. Idea! A bright spark flashed in her mind as she snapped her fingers. Now she knew how to tackle Harshvardhan and get her revenge on him. She stepped out of her bed to go pick up the tabloid that she had cast aside and kept it safely tucked in her handbag. All she had to do was come up with an action plan.

The first thing she planned to do the next day morning was to find out Harshvardhan's schedule for the weekend.

Come morning, it looked like providence was working on her side. There was a news snippet in the day's newspaper about Prince Harshvardhan Singh Gaekwad attending a charity event in Delhi as the chief guest on Saturday evening. Perfect! There was even a mention of the hotel where he was going to stay.

The moment she noticed the movie director Yashwant Mehra at the breakfast buffet, Raksha walked up to him. "Hi Yashwant, good morning," she smiled.

"G'morning, Raksha," said Yashwant, giving her brief smile before continuing to serve himself from the buffet. Harshvardhan had already spoken to him about the incident with the small-time actress the earlier day. The two men went back a long way and had become friends during the shoot of another film a couple of years ago, one that had gone on to become a super success at the box office. Yashwant had a good mind to chuck Raksha Nanda out of the film, especially since she was not adding any value to it. It was just that the pressure from one of the producers was too much. And most of the industry insiders knew about Dhamu Sir and his casting couch.

"Will it be possible for me to have the weekend off? I need to…"

He paused as he was going to add an egg omelette to his plate, looking at her. "That's fine. Keep one of the assistant directors informed." As if it mattered!

"Thanks, Yashwant." Raksha wanted to chat some more with him, but he was already walking away, sitting at a table for four where the other three chairs were already occupied.

Soon, everyone got busy with the shooting while Raksha sat in the background, with nothing to do. The devil had a field day working on her idle mind as she worked on the finer details of her plan.

On the next Monday, Raksha went to a local police station in Delhi, not far from the hotel where Harshvardhan had been staying and filed a FIR—first information report. She wasn't alone as her lawyer had accompanied her. Kamal Desai handed over a typed letter, signed by Raksha, to the inspector-in-charge.

The inspector gestured to them to sit down before reading the three-page letter. The content was all about how the supermodel had been subjected to a high level of embarrassment when the Bollywood star Harshvardhan Singh Gaekwad had tried to sexually molest her.

Inspector Pawan Kumar reached the end of the letter and looked up at Raksha Nanda with shrewd eyes. "Are you sure about this? The man you are accusing of sexual abuse also happens to be the Prince of Baroda. Unless you can prove your case in court, this could land you in big trouble."

Pawan Kumar was one of those good policemen who believed in doing their duty. He also knew a lot about Harshvardhan and his sister Sitara Devi, of the various charities they were a part of. While Princess Sitara Devi did the actual work, her brother also contributed a lot, both financially and by his presence at events. Like, Harshvardhan had been at the charity gala on Saturday, the very day this woman—Raksha Nanda—was accusing him of having sexually abused her.

Raksha looked at her lawyer, giving him a small nod. Kamal Desai cleared his throat before speaking to the inspector. "My client, Ms Raksha Nanda, has undergone a traumatic time at the hands of the actor. You do realise how awkward it is for a lady, especially the supermodel she is, to come out and speak about such an incident? But Ms Nanda has decided that it is time that such people are held responsible for their actions. And that's why she has decided to lodge a complaint. File the FIR immediately, Inspector Pawan Kumar. We need to go to the court to lodge a case against the man immediately after that."

The inspector looked from one to the other before mentally shrugging his shoulders. There wasn't much he could do other than to file the first information report. He took out the form and began asking Raksha a number of questions. She answered each one of them succinctly, without a tremor in her voice.

"Your full name?"

"Raksha Nanda."

"Where do you live?"

She gave him an address in Mumbai.

"What do you do?"

"I'm a fashion model and Bollywood actress."

Pawan looked up at her, wondering why he hadn't seen her in any film and he was such an avid fan of Bollywood. But he refrained from commenting on it, continuing with his questions.

"When did you arrive in Delhi?"

"I came for the weekend. I flew in on Saturday morning and was planning to leave on Sunday evening, that's yesterday. But, well, I decided to stay back to report about Harshvardhan Gaekwad."

"The purpose of your visit?"

"I came to meet an old friend of mine."

"Could you please write out the name, address and contact number of your friend on the back of your letter?" Pawan gave the typed letter to her and watched her pass it on to her lawyer. "Where did you stay?"

She named the 5-star hotel where Harshvardhan had booked a suite.

"Do you personally know Harshvardhan Singh Gaekwad?"

She gave a small nod. "We are both working together on an upcoming film called *Kuch na Kaho*."

"So, what happened on Saturday night?"

"The film-star phoned me in my room and invited me to his suite."

"What time was that? It's okay if you don't have the exact minute in place, but it would be nice if you can give me an approximate time."

"It was past eleven. I know because I had returned to my room only at eleven pm."

Pawan Kumar's gut instinct was that she was too confident and well-rehearsed in her answers—so unlike someone who had undergone trauma, that too, less than forty-eight hours ago. But he kept his thoughts to himself as he continued with his questions.

"What did you do?"

"What?" Raksha frowned at the policeman, having lost the thread of the questions.

"What did you do when he invited you to his suite?" Pawan Kumar repeated his question, adding more clarity.

"What do you think I did? Of course, I refused to go to his suite. It was so late. I'd never visit a strange man in his room even if he is a famous Bollywood star and has a great fan following." There was hatred on Raksha's face.

"Okay. What happened after that?"

"I went to bed. But soon, probably half an hour later, there was a knock on the door. It was him. He walked in… and… and…" She hid her face in her palms, seemingly unable to continue.

"That's the gist of it, Inspector Pawan Kumar. I don't want my client to undergo more trauma than she already has. Now go ahead and file the FIR." Kamal Desai's voice was authoritative as he commanded the police inspector.

Pawan Kumar quickly completed the details on the form, signed it before stamping it. He turned it around towards the lawyer. "Have a look and get Ms Nanda to sign it."

Kamal Desai quickly read the report and handed over his pen for Raksha to sign it, before adding his own signature under witness.

Nodding to Pawan Kumar, the lawyer got up, his hand at Raksha's elbow. "Let's go."

The next morning, Harshvardhan Singh Gaekwad's name once again made headlines on the same tabloid, this time with a picture of a sad but determined looking Raksha Nanda in a long gown of ivory lace, showing her figure to advantage. The headline screamed…

SUPERMODEL TURNED ACTRESS SAYS #METOO

The article carried several quotes from Raksha Nanda. "I'm from a respectable family and keen to make a name in Bollywood. But that doesn't mean that I would stoop to such a level."

The news went on to say, "The film industry is a hotbed of gossip. While the tightly knit community would never betray the villains, we all know that casting couch is very much a part of the industry. Isn't it a good thing that Raksha Nanda, Miss India 2013 finalist and supermodel, has come out in the open as she talks about her traumatic experience at the hands of none other than Prince Harshvardhan Singh Gaekwad who is also a successful Bollywood actor?"

There was a lot more on those lines before it ended with, "We tried to get in touch with Harshvardhan who was unavailable for comment."

People took to social media, using the hashtags #metoo and #nameandshame, being judge and jury as they flung mud against both Harshvardhan and Raksha. News channels went bonkers trying to get a handle on the story, also worried of making a mistake. Nobody could trace the whereabouts of Harshvardhan as he seemed to have disappeared without a trace.

Yashwant had changed the shooting schedule and began to furiously shoot the scenes for which the star was not required. It took a lot of rescheduling but it had to be done.

Harshvardhan had actually gone to Baroda, back to his palace once the news broke out. He was in consultation with his family lawyer, who was doing his best to put together a plan of action.

"But this is simply ridiculous. I was there that night, sharing the suite with Harshvardhan. I can speak on his behalf," said Sitara Devi, sparks of fury flying from her eyes as she spoke to the lawyer. Not easily roused to anger, she was beyond furious on her brother's behalf. More so since she simply could not tolerate this kind of false accusations.

Vishal Trivedi, their lawyer, sat in front of them, calmly sipping from his cup of coffee, thinking over the matter. Keeping his empty cup down, he spoke to Sitara Devi, "We don't know yet if this model will actually file a case. Even if she does, your evidence as the defendant's sister won't carry much weight. We will need to tackle this correctly, gather public confidence as we go." He turned to Harshvardhan and said, "It is best that you give a press release and maybe put up a post on your Facebook and Twitter accounts stating the truth. Don't take that woman's name. Just say that you have done nothing to be ashamed of."

Harshvardhan nodded. When his phone began to ring non-stop, he had switched it off, not wanting to answer stupid questions, making all calls from the palace landline. Following the lawyer's instruction, he had a press release given through his PR agency.

After that, he went up to the terrace and sat on the wall, deep in thought. What would Dayanita think about him after reading this news piece? She hadn't been in touch with him since the time she left his home on Thursday morning. Today was Tuesday. When he heard about the news early in the morning, Harshvardhan had called Yashwant to cancel the shoot before taking a flight to Baroda. He felt that he had to get away from it all, a peace haven where he could think clearly.

He really could do without something like this at this point in his career. He was a famous film-star but still had a long way to go before becoming a superstar. But he had been—was—working towards it.

The #metoo movement had brought to light people who harassed others in the name of sex, not just in the film industry but also in other industries. Recently, there had been an article by veteran actress Daisy Rani who had begun her film career as a small girl. She had openly spoken of being sexually exploited by not one, but many men from the Hindi film industry. But the people she named were no more.

But now, Raksha Nanda had taken an extra step, to falsely accuse him of sexual harassment. The main problem was that the law leaned more towards the women in such cases. Damn it all! Harshvardhan jumped off the wall to walk up and down the terrace. That woman was trouble with a capital T. And it was she who had tried to sexually exploit him. The other day in his vanity van, she had pressed close to his body and even tried to kiss him. What a bitch! Unless he came up with some concrete evidence that he had been where he actually was, he might land in deep shit.

Harshvardhan felt like kicking something, hard. He and Yashwant had agreed to postpone the shooting until such time something could be done about the situation. The inaction was terrible. He came a quick decision and rushed down to talk to Sitara.

"*Di*, I'm off to our Hazira palace. I need to lie low and I don't want your work affected because of my presence here. I…"

She looked at him with anxious eyes, saying, "Don't be silly, Harsh. You should stay here. I…"

"It's for the best. I want to be alone. I have a lot of thinking to do. Somehow, I need to crack this case and believe me, I plan to sue that bitch for defamation and make her pay through her nose."

A small smile broke out on Sitara's face on hearing his words. "Absolutely, Harsh. And that tabloid too."

He nodded. "So, I'll take off now. One thing, *di*…" he hesitated. Was it fair to leave her to face the press? They would definitely land here soon. He sighed before continuing, "The press will land up here soon. I don't want you to face them alone. I…"

"Don't you worry about that. I'll let Rituraj handle them. And they will leave, once they know that you aren't here."

He gave his sister a hug. "Thanks, *di*. I plan to keep my phone switched off. We'll be in touch via the landline there."

She nodded, giving him a worried glance as he left to go pack for his trip.

Harshvardhan sat in his car and took his wallet out to look for the single earring that he had salvaged from where it had been lying in The Beverly Hills Hotel. Dayanita's silver earring set with pink tourmaline. When, at first, he had felt betrayed by her, he had simply tossed the earring in his luggage, planning to courier it to her. But later, he had held on to it, not liking the idea of parting with something that belonged to the love of his life. Many times, he had held it like a talisman in his hand, whenever he felt that they might not get together.

But, where was the earring? He frowned, removing all the cash and cards from his wallet, turning it upside down before shaking it. But the earring wasn't there any longer. Was it an omen? He had had it till yesterday, hadn't he? He scowled some more. When had he seen it last?

Thinking for a long time, totally distracted from his immediate problems, Harshvardhan wondered when he had seen Dayanita's earring last. At the Delhi hotel? Now he remembered taking the earring in his hand and holding it as he lay on the bed, sending one more message of love to the real princess.

He must have gone to sleep holding it in his hand and could not recall putting the earring back in his wallet after that. He must have forgotten it on the bed as they had checked out soon after waking up. Shit! More than the earring, it was his connection with Dayanita.

Now was not the right time to get in touch with the hotel. But they had an excellent reputation. He was confident that they would keep the earring safe. He would just have to be patient about it.

Harshvardhan banged his fist on the steering wheel in frustration. He was totally running out of patience, with every damn thing—his career as well as his girlfriend. Now, with the latest issue that had sprung up, the rest of his life seemed to have been put on hold.

What a snarl!

The Delhi hotel called Sitara Devi sometime after Harshvardhan had left for Hazira. "Princess Sitara Devi? I'm calling from the Marriott, Delhi. We found an earring in one of the bedrooms of the suite you were staying at. Would you like us to courier it to you?"

Sitara Devi frowned at the phone, unable to recall losing an earring during the trip. Anyway, she was too distracted to grasp what the man was saying as she turned to her secretary and said, "Will you take this call, Rituraj?"

Rituraj listened to the manager for a few minutes before saying, "Could you please keep the earring safe for the princess? We'll give you a call regarding the same."

Neither of them realised how important the earring was to Harshvardhan and forgot all about it.

19

ayanita woke up to check her phone for any messages from Harshvardhan. She was enjoying herself thoroughly, looking forward to his many messages through the day, though not bothering to answer them.

All that soul searching the earlier day had been a temporary activity. She had forgotten all about it and was having fun at his expense. Well, she didn't think that he really minded. If that were the case, he wouldn't be continuing to send her those messages, would he?

Tch! She was disappointed that there was nothing from him today. Getting up to stretch, she got ready for the day. Today, she planned to polish up her script a bit more and send it to a couple of film companies. She had hoped that her script would be selected as one of the top three at the film academy that Harshvardhan had promised to find producers for. But no such luck! Shawn was a lucky dog indeed. He was one of the three finalists and hadn't stopped crowing from the time the announcement had been made.

Quickly dressing up in a calf-length skirt and top in brilliant orange and green, Dayanita rushed down the staircase to walk into the dining room. "Good morning, guys," she called out cheerfully before sitting down on a chair and pouring herself a cup of coffee from the flask. When there was no answer from even one of the members of her family, she looked up with raised eyebrows. "What's up?"

Her mother, Ragini Devi, appeared teary-eyed, while her father, Gajendar, gave her an anxious look. Her sisters-in-law didn't meet her eyes as they seemed to concentrate on their food. She turned to look at Indrajeet and Rajvardhan to ask, "Is something the issue? Isn't Grandma keeping well?"

Indrajeet spoke. "Not Grandma, Nita. Er… there's this news item that has come out…"

"Is it about Harsh?" she asked. When he nodded, she said, "Where's the paper?"

Rajvardhan handed her the tabloid without uttering a word. In fact, everyone kept their silence as Dayanita read through the article. Without a change in her expression, she crushed the paper and threw it on the empty chair next to hers, saying, "That's just crap. My Harsh would *never* do such a thing."

Both Gajendar and Ragini lost their anxious looks as they both smiled on hearing their daughter's words.

Her brothers laughed in relief, while Yashodhara and Chitrangada looked up and smiled. "I'm so glad to hear you say that, Nita," said Indrajeet, adding another *kachori* to his plate.

"We've been really worried about your reaction," said Rajvardhan. "It's not that we believe that

Harshvardhan is capable of it. He's too nice a guy. But you have not been…"

"…in touch with him. But that's not true, Raj. It's true that I haven't been talking to him. But he's been in touch with me all along."

"That guy sure deserves sainthood," said Indrajeet, shaking his head at his sister.

"Jeet! Let me assure you that Harsh is a completely unsuitable candidate for sainthood. By the way, did you speak to him today, Raj?"

Rajvardhan sighed. "His phone is switched off."

She grimaced. "The paparazzi! Shit! They must be hounding him. I want to talk to him. How can I do that?" She looked from Indrajeet to Rajvardhan, hoping that they would come up with a solution.

"I can call his sister Sitara Devi…" Rajvardhan offered, lifting his eyebrow at her.

"Could you? Will you ask her how to get in touch with Harsh?"

"Do you want to speak to her?" he asked, dialling Sitara Devi's cell number.

She shook her head, not saying anything when it became obvious that the call had been picked up at the other end.

"Hello, Princess Sitara, this is Rajvardhan Thakore. I'm trying to get in touch with Harsh, but his phone is switched off."

"Hello, Rajvardhan. Harshvardhan is on his way here. I'll ask him to give you a call when he reaches home."

That had been in the morning. Now it was past six in the evening and there still had been no communication from Harshvardhan. Dayanita's mood swung between anxiety and anger as she thought about the man she had fallen in love with.

As Indrajeet had mentioned, Harshvardhan definitely deserved sainthood, the way she had been trying his patience from the moment they had met. Dayanita sighed. But what could she do? She seemed to have no control over her temper. But then again, he didn't seem to mind at all and actually loved her despite all that.

But why hadn't he called her? Rajvardhan had left a message with Sitara Devi. She grimaced, wondering if the situation was worse than what it was. Harshvardhan's shooting schedule ran all seven days of the week. She knew from Rajvardhan that he was going to take an off on the coming Thursday after two whole weeks of work. But he had obviously dropped his shooting schedule to go home to Baroda. She sat up straight on the sofa. She had thought too lightly of the news. What if Harshvardhan was in trouble because of that woman's accusations? Jumping up from her seat, Dayanita went in search of Rajvardhan, calling out his name loudly.

"Hey, sis. What's up?" he asked, walking in from the garden where he had been helping Gajendar plant some fruit trees.

"Will you take me to Baroda? I…" She gave him a nervous look before continuing, "I don't want to go there alone." It won't be just Harshvardhan she would be meeting there, but also his sister, Sitara Devi.

Dayanita was worried of creating a bad impression at their first meeting.

Rajvardhan had been thinking along the same lines. Sitara Devi had mentioned that her brother was going home. Since contacting him on phone didn't seem to be working, it was best to go meet him personally. There may be a snag though. There may be newspaper reporters hounding his residence. If that were the case, it didn't make sense dragging Dayanita into the midst of it.

"I don't mind taking you, Nita. But shall we wait until tomorrow? I…"

"Please Raj." Dayanita had never had to plead for anything in her life before. But she was desperate to meet Harshvardhan and tell him, no, show him that he had her support.

Rajvardhan shook his head. "Listen, the paparazzi is bound to be hanging outside the palace. It might become messy if you land amidst them. I don't think you really care what they print about you, but it should not make Harshvardhan's case worse than it already is."

Dayanita paled on hearing his words, nodding her head slowly. "You're right. But please can we go as soon as you think it's safe?" She held his arm; a beseeching look on her face.

Rajvardhan patted his little sister's cheek. "No worries, sis. We'll go as soon as we can."

Kiran spat his coffee when he read the tabloid headline. What the fuck! Had Raksha named Dhamu Sir in the article? Even if she had mentioned it to the newspaper correspondent, will they have dared to print the producer's name? He quickly read the article, visibly relaxing when he reached the end. She had named Harshvardhan, and not Dhamu Sir as he had been worried about. To be truthful, Kiran had been scared that his name might also have been dragged into the muck.

Phew!

But, how had Harshvardhan got entangled in this mess? Kiran knew everyone in the film industry, all because he made it a point to gather information. It had helped him a lot in his business of helping young women get into movies. There had even been a couple of lucky ones who had made it big too.

As far as he knew, Harshvardhan was a loner who kept to himself. While he attended parties where he needed to be present, he usually left early. Women flocked him, most definitely. And why not? After all, he was handsome and well built, his films doing very well at the box office. But that didn't mean that he encouraged them. He was a man driven by ambition, passionate about his career. He was twenty-nine and probably had been in a few relationships. But there was no steady girlfriend. Kiran recalled the article a few days ago, on this same tabloid, with a picture of a princess from Udaipur. But all that was speculation, with no concrete basis.

In the meanwhile, Raksha was not just ambitious, but ready to stoop to any level to get a role in

Bollywood. She had landed one too. Kiran frowned, thinking hard. And it had been in a film backed by Dhamu Sir. He snapped his fingers. Harshvardhan was the hero in that film which was tentatively titled *Kuch na Kaho*.

What had Raksha been doing in Delhi in the middle of the shooting schedule? Harshvardhan had had a valid reason of being a chief guest at a charity event organised by his sister. Otherwise, the actor was a thorough professional, never having cancelled a schedule till date.

Thoughts churned in his mind as Kiran got ready for work. His phone rang just as he was getting on his scooty. He grimaced when he saw that it was from Dhamu Sir. "Good morning, Dhamu Sir. How have you been?"

The producer started yelling immediately. "Kiran, it's a bad morning for you as I'm wondering what would be the best way to dispose you off. That cunt you brought me last month… she's coughed to a newspaper. How could you do this to me? I'm…"

Kiran gave a nervous laugh. "No, Dhamu Sir. Listen to me. This is about Raksha, right? She's not taken your name in the newspaper. She…"

"That's not the point. She…"

"No, sir. She has named Harshvardhan, even giving a date and venue. She…"

Dhamu Sir's voice rose up to a crescendo, keen to blame Kiran for what he believed to be his predicament. "You listen to me, Kiran… what? What did you say?"

Kiran laughed softly. "You heard me, Dhamu Sir. This issue is something entirely different."

"Hmm… alright. But just keep a lookout, okay? This woman is dangerous. What she has done to Harshvardhan today, she could do to you and me tomorrow."

Kiran grimaced, in total agreement with the producer's words. "I will, sir. But today you can be at peace."

"That's right," said Dhamu Sir, cutting the call, not bothering to say 'bye'. Kiran was, after all, a pimp. Why bother?!

Harshvardhan called his sister the moment he entered their palace in Hazira. "Hey *di*. I've reached."

Sitara Devi sighed. "Just in time too, Harsh. The newshounds have gathered around our palace. They began to arrive barely within half an hour of your departure. I'm so glad you left when you did. Rituraj is dealing with them as we talk."

Harshvardhan laughed softly. "Whoa! Talk about a lucky escape. But sorry that I left you to deal with them, *di*." There was regret in his voice.

"Shuddup, little bro. I'm not going to let you face this all alone. I'm your bossy elder sis, remember?"

He laughed again. "I do, I do. And I'm so glad for it. And *di,* you must come over when you can. This place is so amazing. Brijmohan and Nirupama have maintained it so well too."

"We'll go there together sometime soon, after this mess blows over."

A deep sigh shuddered through Harshvardhan. "I'll catch you soon, *di.*" He placed the receiver down on the antique silver telephone etched with the face of a horse in the centre of the old-fashioned dial, before walking up the wooden staircase to the master bedroom that used to belong to his parents. He had a shower before going down to the dining room where Brijmohan served him with a three-course meal that had been prepared by Nirupama.

"*Kunwarji*, may I serve you one more *naan*?" Brijmohan offered respectfully.

Harshvardhan shook his head, smiling. "No, no. If you feed me like this, I will put on so much weight that I wouldn't be able to play the hero in another film."

Brijmohan looked sheepish as he grinned back at his young master. He had been working for the Gaekwad family since he was twelve years old, way before even Sitara Devi was born.

"Briju, do you want to watch my latest movie?" Harshvardhan asked suddenly, looking at the loyal servant.

Brijmohan's face lit up with a bright smile. "We'd love to."

"Right. Let me set up the screen. You and Nirupama have your dinner and come fast."

"*Ji, Kunwarji,*" said Brijmohan, rushing back to the kitchen where his wife was making hot *naans.*

In half an hour, they sat down in front of the 75-inch LED TV to watch *Pyar se Takrar,* a rom-com starring

Harshvardhan that had released six months ago. It was still running to full houses in some suburban theatres.

As the end credits ran, Brijmohan turned back to tell Harshvardhan how much they had enjoyed the movie only to find the prince fast asleep as he lay back on the sofa. The servant got up to switch the TV off before bringing a comforter down from the bedroom to spread it over the sleeping prince before taking off to his quarters at the back.

ituraj stepped out of the outhouse—actually a two thousand square-foot bungalow built in two storeys in the same compound as the Gaekwad palace—at six in the morning to go for his regular jog and was surprised to sight a few people hanging out near the ornate gates. There were even a couple of TV vans parked nearby.

Damn it! It looked like these people didn't have any other juicy news to run on their channels. He had been polite but firm when he had dealt with the lot the earlier night, telling them clearly that Harshvardhan was not in the palace. But obviously some of them hadn't really believed him. He was amazed at their persistence. Shrugging mentally, he opened the gate, after waving to the security guard who sat in his cabin, before stepping out.

The hounds pounced on him the next instant, thrusting their mikes against his face. "I want to meet Prince Harshvardhan urgently," said one.

"Is he in the palace?"

"Where is he?"

"Has he fled the country?"

"My channel is keen to present his side of the story."

Suddenly, instead of the few people he had thought he had seen, Rituraj found himself surrounded by at least twenty reporters. He lifted a hand to stop the chatter and waited for complete silence before talking. "Prince Harshvardhan is not here. And I don't really know where he is. You guys are simply wasting your time here."

"Who are you?"

"Do you live on the premises?"

"How are you connected to the royal family?"

Rituraj laughed out loud. "You guys are really something. Where do you get the energy so early in the morning? My name is Rituraj Srivastava. I'm Princess Sitara Devi's personal assistant. I live in the outhouse." He raised a hand when they would have asked him more questions. "I lead a boring life that will surely not get you any TRPs. Bye folks!" He waved to them as he slowly began to jog away from the area.

When he returned an hour and ten kilometres later, the people as well as the vans had disappeared. Phew!

That morning, a copy of the court summons was delivered to the palace, instructing Harshvardhan to present himself for a hearing at the Delhi High Court. Because of the high-profile nature of the people involved in the case, the matter had been expedited and brought forward to be heard on the coming Monday.

"That's less than a week," said Sitara Devi, a worried look on her face.

Rituraj nodded, not saying anything in reply. What was there to say?!

After tossing and turning through a sleepless night, Dayanita was up and ready at seven in the morning. She draped a silk sari of pastel green, teamed with a long-sleeved blouse and matching jewellery. After all, she had to create an impression as she was going to meet the woman who was going to be her sister-in-law soon.

She went down to get some coffee and was glad to see that Rajvardhan was also up. "All set to go, sis?" When she nodded, he said, "I called Sitara Devi's assistant and he says the coast is clear with no newspaper people around."

"Perfect." She raised a hand in a high-five before asking eagerly, "Shall we leave now?"

Taking pity on his little sister, Rajvardhan nodded. "Yep. As soon as I finish my coffee."

They left immediately after, driving to the airport before taking off in their private plane that was all ready and waiting for them.

"Welcome," said Rituraj, meeting the duo at the door, shaking Rajvardhan's hand.

"This is my sister, Princess Dayanita Thakore. And Dayanita, this is Rituraj Srivastava, Her Royal Highness Sitara Devi's personal assistant."

Dayanita nodded her head regally, giving the other man a small smile, her eyes searching behind him for Harshvardhan, disappointed at not finding him there.

"Please be seated, the princess should come down in a few minutes. She hopes you will join her for breakfast."

"And Harsh? Is he up?" asked Dayanita, totally impatient.

Rituraj smiled at her, replying, "The prince isn't here, ma'am."

"What?" Dayanita jumped up from the sofa she had been sitting on, turning shocked eyes to her brother before shifting her piercing gaze to the other man. "Where is he, then?"

"That's not for me to tell, ma'am. If you will be seated, please? As I said, the princess... she's here," he said, relief in his voice when he noticed Sitara Devi at the top of the staircase.

Rajvardhan got up too, walking forward to shake Sitara Devi's hand when she stepped down into the hall. "Good morning, Princess Sitara."

"Good morning, Prince Rajvardhan," she responded, her smile not reaching her eyes.

Rajvardhan performed the introductions yet again, now between Sitara Devi and Dayanita.

Dayanita's eyes were shimmering with unshed tears as she looked at Harshvardhan's sister. They had the exact same eyes. She moved suddenly, to throw her arms around the older woman, hugging her close. "I'm so sorry about this mess," she whispered in a choked voice.

Rajvardhan stared in surprise, having difficulty in holding his sagging jaw. He had never seen this side of Dayanita in all her life.

Sitara Devi's smile brightened as she returned the Thakore princess's hug with equal enthusiasm, patting her gently on her back, before sighing softly.

Dayanita stepped back to stare at Sitara. "How is Harsh? Where is he?"

"Why don't we talk at the breakfast table?" Sitara Devi turned towards the dining hall, gesturing for them to follow.

Dayanita gave her an impatient look but refrained from saying anything as she took Rajvardhan's hand and followed in her wake.

Sitting down to breakfast, Sitara Devi told them the exact details of the sordid story, helped along by Rituraj.

"So, it's like this. Our lawyer says that my words, as Harsh's sister, will hold no good in a court of law. I…"

"But that's only the truth. How can they not accept it?" Dayanita interrupted, pushing away her plate from which she had eaten but a few bites, too upset by what she was hearing.

Sitara Devi's smile was affectionate this time as she eyed the young lady her brother had fallen in love with. "You are right, Nita. I may call you Nita, right?" She continued when Dayanita gave her an impatient nod, "But that's how the judiciary system works. And just now, we received a court summons for Harsh. He is to appear for a hearing in Delhi on Monday."

Not responding to her, Dayanita got up to walk out of the dining room, her mind working furiously. There had to be a way out. If the court cannot accept the truth, then how can it accept the lie that that Raksha woman was perpetrating? It was so unfair. Deep down in her heart, Dayanita knew that Harshvardhan would never assault anyone, sexually or otherwise.

She turned around suddenly and walked back to ask Sitara Devi, "Where is Harsh now? Is he safe? I mean, is he safe from the newshounds?"

"Yes, he is. He's gone to our palace at Hazira."

"Oh, but he must be so lonely!" cried Dayanita, her eyes stinging with unshed tears. "I… may I please go there?" She looked at Sitara Devi pathetically.

Sitara Devi got up to walk to Dayanita, throwing an arm around her shoulders. "I understand you, Nita. But it's best that Harsh is left alone. For one thing, he wants to be by himself. For another, we don't want anyone to nose out his hiding place. I did offer to go along with him. But he refused."

But he wouldn't say 'no' to me. Dayanita was sure of it. She decided not to argue though. Sitara Devi must be anxious about her brother's situation without her adding to it.

"I have been thinking…" Dayanita looked up to see if Rajvardhan was with them as she talked about her plan. "The court will not accept your words since you are Harsh's sister. But what if I swear in court that he was with me the whole night?"

Sitara Devi's eyes went wide as she stared at the young Thakore princess, while a slow smile spread over Rajvardhan's face as he gave his sister a proud look.

"Go for it, Nita. I'll back your claim. Actually, all of us Thakores can go to court while you swear to this. The judge as well as the public will have no choice but to believe you."

"But... but it will be Nita's reputation at stake," said Sitara Devi, looking from brother to sister and back again, totally shocked by their words.

"Sitara *di*, will you not bless my marriage to Harsh if I gain a soiled reputation?" asked Dayanita, tongue in cheek as she gave Sitara Devi a mischievous look. The tears had disappeared to give way to a look of battle in her eyes.

Sitara Devi burst out laughing, reminding Dayanita so much of Harshvardhan who laughed in exactly the same fashion.

"Has Harsh proposed to wed you yet?" asked the Gaekwad princess, eyeing the younger woman with dancing eyes.

Dayanita shook her head slowly. "No. But I'll propose to him for sure. For, I'll have to make an honest man of him after that declaration in court, right?"

Sitara laughed again, highly amused, especially as she felt the death grip of fear easing from her heart. Her brother stood a chance at winning the case now. "Let me call the lawyer."

"Yes, please. And we also need to get our story together, the day, date, venue and all that."

"Have you done this before, Nita?" It was Sitara's turn to tease now as she asked Dayanita.

Dayanita grinned, shaking her head. "I did a one-year course at script-writing. They teach the students to think in logical steps."

"Perfect. Rituraj, call Vishal and ask him to come ASAP. And let's go and get our story together, Nita. If you'll join us, Raj? We could do with a third-party view as well as a male viewpoint."

"But, of course," said Rajvardhan, giving his sister a hug. Today, his respect for Dayanita had gone up by several notches.

The two princesses got together, Dayanita taking notes on her phone, getting their act together to save the man they loved.

21

The Thakore family along with Sitara Devi, had moved into the same hotel in Delhi on Sunday afternoon before the hearing. Harshvardhan was to fly in on Monday morning and go directly to the court for the ten o'clock hearing.

He still did not know that Dayanita was going to testify on his behalf. That had been decided on the lawyer's advice as Vishal Trivedi did not want the news to get out. It was a good thing that no one was aware of the Thakore family's involvement.

The minute Sitara Devi and Dayanita had settled down in the suite that they were sharing, there was a knock on the door. The manager walked in, handing a small velvet pouch to the Gaekwad princess reverently. Sitara remembered the phone call from the hotel and opened the pouch to stare at the earring, not recognising it.

Before she could say anything, Dayanita squealed, "That's mine. How did it get here? I had lost it…" She clamped up, not saying anymore.

Sitara Devi dismissed the manager with a royal nod before turning to smile at Dayanita. "What happened, Nita? You were saying?"

"I left the earring in Harshvardhan's suite at The Beverly Hills Hotel in Los Angeles," she said in a soft voice, looking Sitara Devi squarely in the eye.

Sitara Devi's brows came together as she tried to grasp the meaning of it. "I suppose Harsh must have had it with him and had left it here in the hotel by mistake." She couldn't think of any other logical explanation to it.

Dayanita snapped her fingers, an expression of delight on her face. "Sitara *di*, listen, this is the best thing that could have happened." She quickly explained what she meant to Sitara before the latter got in touch with the lawyer who had also come to Delhi with them and was staying in the same hotel.

Vishal Trivedi arrived within five minutes. Quickly the three of them put their heads together and came up with a plan.

"I'll handle everything, Princess Sitara. This is Godsend, the answer to all your prayers. There's no way that Harshvardhan can't win the case." The lawyer left to do the needful.

Dayanita's whole family, including *Rajmata* Santhini Devi, her parents, her brothers and sisters-in-law went ahead and settled down in the courtroom where the hearing was to take place. Only Aditya was left back at the hotel with his nurse. They managed to get seats despite the crowd as they had arrived well before nine.

Sitara Devi went separately along with Rituraj, not acknowledging the Thakore family as she seated herself in the front row where two chairs had been kept empty for them.

As again instructed by Vishal Trivedi, Dayanita wore a cream-coloured burqa with a mesh over her eyes which enabled her to see. She travelled to the court by herself and slid into a seat at the back, careful not to draw attention to herself.

It was ten minutes to ten when Harshvardhan walked into the court, removing the monkey cap and glares that had served as an excellent disguise. A couple of policemen stopped some members of the paparazzi when they tried to shove their microphones under the Bollywood star's prominent nose.

Dayanita watched on, admiring his proud stance as Harshvardhan walked forward to sit next to his lawyer. He had lost weight while his face displayed no smile. *I'll get that smile back on his face today*, she swore to herself.

Raksha Nanda arrived soon after on her lawyer's arm, wearing a stark red figure-hugging dress that stopped an inch short of her knees, paired with three-inch heels of the same colour.

Dayanita smiled widely, not bothered about what others might think since her face was well-covered by her burqa. If the supermodel was into power dressing, her costume was definitely a fail. The idiot obviously was not aware of how the Indian public reacted to such clothes. But, it only made Dayanita's life easier. It would not be difficult to establish Raksha Nanda as a scarlet woman wanting to get her claws into the Bollywood hero.

The judge arrived, beating the gavel on his desk to bring silence to the courtroom before he called out to the prosecuting lawyer to make his statement.

Kamal Desai got up from his seat to make a long drawn out speech regarding the manner in which his client had been molested on that particular Saturday night at the Delhi hotel. He made Raksha Nanda take the stand. She was sworn in before he asked her a lot of questions, bringing the whole matter to light or that was what they were trying to establish.

Dayanita fumed as she awaited her turn. Once Kamal Desai had completed his side of the case, Vishal Trivedi got up to present the defendant's side.

Harshvardhan was sworn in when he took the stand, answering his lawyer's questions concisely and truthfully, without a tremor in his voice. He showed no anger or bitterness and Dayanita was all admiration for him at the end of it. During cross-examination, Kamal Desai tried his best to make the actor admit to something that he had not done. But Harshvardhan maintained his stand. "I never phoned the model's room nor did I visit her, not on that night, not ever."

"I would like to call on a witness at this stage, my lord." Vishal had lifted a hand to her and Dayanita was already walking down the aisle when the lawyer made the statement.

"You may proceed," said the judge, gazing in surprise at the burqa-clad woman.

"Princess Dayanita Thakore." Vishal Trivedi presented her with a flourish as she took the stand, removing her burqa and standing straight, royal to the core in a silk sari the colour of sandalwood, her makeup understated while the Thakore family diamonds flashed in her ears and at her throat.

The judge had to bring his gavel down several times before silence reigned as all those present were chatting at once, the surprise evident on their faces. It was only after seeing Dayanita take the stand that the reporters noticed her family present in the court. All this long, they had been completely focused on Harshvardhan and making plans to snatch him the moment it became possible.

Dayanita took the oath to speak the truth and nothing but the truth. She had made peace with her conscience. She was going to tell a lie to beat Raksha's lie. The truth was that Harshvardhan was innocent of the evil's woman's accusations. But there was no provision in the law to help him in this case. He was her better half and it was up to her to save him from this situation. So, what if they were not married? She loved him and had accepted him as her life partner. Everything else was but a formality.

Vishal Trivedi walked close to the witness stand and asked his questions.

"Your name?"

"Dayanita Thakore."

"Do you know the defendant, Harshvardhan Singh Gaekwad?"

"Yes, I do." She looked into Harshvardhan's eyes when she made that statement, smiling at his shocked face.

"Where and when did you meet him for the first time?"

"In Los Angeles." She gave the month and date three months ago. "He had come to give a lecture at the film academy where I was studying."

"Have you met each other subsequently?"

"Many times."

"On this particular Saturday…" Vishal Trivedi looked down at the papers in his hand and announced the date of the weekend before last, continuing, "Where were you?"

"Objection, my lord! That amounts to leading the witness," Kamal Desai sprang from his chair to protest.

"Let me reframe the question," said Vishal Trivedi, even before the judge could say anything. "Can you tell the court about the relationship you share with the defendant?"

"We are in a live-in relationship." The court was in an uproar as the people couldn't believe their ears. She was from a royal household. And he was a prince. How did she have the guts to make such an announcement in public? Her reputation would be in shreds now.

Harshvardhan looked at Dayanita with adoring eyes. He had caught on by now what she and the lawyer were trying to establish. He turned to look at his sister who gave him an encouraging nod. And then there were the members of Dayanita's family who were all present, even the *Rajmata*. Talk about solidarity! Further beyond, he noticed Yashwant sitting on a chair and smiled at his director. They were all here to stand by his side. Wasn't he so lucky!

It took the judge a few minutes to bring order. "If there's no silence in ten seconds, I'll have the court cleared before continuing with the case," he said sternly as he glared at the people present. The audience became silent within a few seconds.

"Do you meet regularly?" Vishal Trivedi continued with his questions.

Dayanita shrugged. "Not regularly as Harshvardhan is extremely busy with his shoot. I returned from the USA only recently. I went to meet him in Karjat when I got back. It was even in the papers," she said, laughing softly as she looked at the audience gathered there, many of them Harshvardhan's fans, meeting random people's eyes boldly. She needed them on her side. They had been shocked by her statement but were slowly warming up to her. And she had the right power dressing too! She smiled maliciously when her eyes fell on Raksha who was scowling heavily by now.

"We meet at random times. I stayed at his bungalow in Mumbai for some time. He's even been to meet my family. By the way, they are all here," she said, gesturing towards the Thakores as she spoke directly to the judge. She was only telling the truth, wasn't she? Only they did not have to know that he had visited her people even before she returned to India.

People craned their necks to catch a glimpse of Dayanita's family. In their eyes, her reputation had taken on a different aspect altogether now.

"And?" Vishal Trivedi prodded, giving her a small nod. It was time to nail the case now.

"The last time we met was in Delhi. When I got to know that Harshvardhan was taking a break on Saturday to attend the charity event organised by his sister, Princess Sitara Devi Gaekwad, I decided to surprise him there. I booked into the same hotel for the night and… and," Dayanita blushed naturally as she lowered her voice deliberately to say, "Sitara Devi spent the night in my room while I stayed with Harshvardhan in the suite they had booked for the two of them."

Pandemonium broke out in the court as the crowd roared, everyone on the lovers' side by now. The lowered voice and secretive tone had struck the perfect note as each person had strained to catch her words. Many of the news reporters rushed from the court to get their stories out as they vied for being the first ones to do so.

The judge looked on the scene with a small smile on his face, appearing like Father Christmas as he waited for everyone to calm down.

Kamal Desai spoke the moment silence reigned. "She's lying."

"That was out of turn, prosecutor," reprimanded the judge, his smile wiped off as his expression turned grim. "You will get your chance to cross-examine the witness for defence."

"I'm done, my lord. The witness is ready for cross-examination," said Vishal Trivedi, a benign smile on his face. Princess Dayanita Thakore had played her part to perfection. There was no chance of Harshvardhan losing the case. The lawyer went to sit on his chair and patted his client's shoulder, giving him a thumbs-up.

Kamal Desai tried to break Dayanita's story by throwing unexpected and random questions at her. And Vishal Trivedi didn't even bother to raise an objection as the Thakore Princess was more than capable of dealing with Raksha's lawyer.

Dayanita was bold with just a trace of arrogance as she answered the prosecution lawyer's questions, never deviating from her story, not once.

Kamal Desai called Princess Sitara Devi to the stand and asked her a number of questions. But all her answers matched those of Princess Dayanita one hundred percent. Finally giving up, he went back to sit in his chair, refusing to look at Raksha Nanda's angry face.

"There's one last witness that I want to call from the defendant's side, my lord," said Vishal Trivedi, looking up at the judge.

"You may proceed," said the judge while Kamal Desai glared at the opposition lawyer, wondering what else the other man had up his sleeve. Hadn't he done enough to tear the case apart?

The Marriott Hotel manager came and took the stand and was sworn in. After answering a number of questions, he identified the single pink tourmaline earring that the lawyer took out of his coat pocket, in front of the court and said, "This earring was found in the suite where Princess Sitara Devi and Prince Harshvardhan Gaekwad had stayed on the particular Saturday night. The cleaning staff found it and handed it to me on Sunday after the guests had checked out."

"What did you do after that?"

"I called Sitara Devi at her palace to tell her about it. Her secretary instructed me that we should keep the earring safe until further instructions. Yesterday, when the princess checked into our hotel again, I personally handed the earring to her."

"Thank you, you may go," said Vishal Trivedi when Kamal Desai didn't show any interest in cross-examining the hotel manager.

Vishal Trivedi called Princess Sitara Devi back on the stand. Once she denied that the earring belonged to her, he made Harshvardhan take the stand. "Do you know who this earring belongs to?"

Harshvardhan smiled, having completely understood what was happening. After all, that piece of jewellery had again proved to be his talisman. "That earring belongs to Princess Dayanita Thakore."

"And that," concluded Vishal Trivedi, "proves beyond doubt that my client, Prince Harshvardhan Singh Gaekwad had spent the night with Princess Dayanita Thakore and not with Ms Raksha Nanda as the prosecution claims."

The uproar this time did not die till the judge called for a ten-minute recess. "I'll return with my judgement by then."

More reporters made urgent calls to their offices while Dayanita went to sit with Sitara Devi, holding her hand tightly in hers. She refused to look in Harshvardhan's direction because of her fear of breaking down in tears if she met his gaze.

Indrajeet and Rajvardhan rushed over to pull Dayanita out of her seat and hug her. "You were brilliant, sis," said Indrajeet in a whisper. "All this long I was thinking that you are so lucky to have

Harshvardhan for your life partner. Today, I know for a fact that he's absolutely lucky to have you."

Rajvardhan grinned at her too, saying, "You killed it, sis."

She nodded, not uttering a word, her throat feeling choked. She would be at peace only after the verdict was out. For all of everyone's confidence, she couldn't help the trace of fear that continued to dog her.

The judge returned exactly ten minutes later, bringing silence to the court immediately, all faces turned eagerly towards him as they waited for his judgement.

"In the case of Raksha Nanda vs Harshvardhan Singh Gaekwad, I pronounce the defendant completely innocent of all charges..." He paused when most of the people got up as one to roar their approval, some even clapping loudly. After a two-minute wait brought no solace, the judge banged his gavel extra loudly. "I know there are a number of Harshvardhan's fans in the audience, but that doesn't mean that you are all above the law. Would you rather I threw you all out? Or maybe levied a fine in contempt of court?"

The crowd quietened down, though not completely, just enough for the full judgement to be heard. "To continue, I pronounce Harshvardhan Singh Gaekwad completely innocent of all charges made against him. I also recommend that he lodges a defamation case against Ms Nanda as well as the media houses that have defiled his name. In the meanwhile, I order Ms Nanda to pay a fine of Rs 50,000 to the court for filing false allegations against the defendant." He signed the judgement copies, handing them over to both the legal counsels before leaving the courtroom.

Dayanita left Sitara's side and flew into Harshvardhan's arms, burying her face in his shoulder, her body trembling in reaction as she couldn't stop the tears from flowing. "I love you, Harsh. I love you more than my life," she said, lifting her face to kiss him on his lips.

"I always knew that, babe. Will you make an honest man of me now that you have declared to the whole world that we are living in sin?" He grinned as he pressed his forehead to hers, wiping her tears away with both his hands.

"Not in sin. Never in sin. Our lovemaking is something too beautiful," she said, kissing him once again.

"But you haven't answered my question, Nita," he growled in her ear.

"And what was that?" she asked, raising a supercilious brow, even as her eyes shone with her love for him.

He removed his arms away from her body to move back a couple of steps before going on his knee. Phones flashed as many took pictures of the moment when the prince of Baroda asked the princess of Udaipur, "Will you marry me?"

"Yes, my Harsh," she said, throwing her arms around his neck and hugging him close.

Sitara Devi threw her arms around her brother and his *fiancée*, hugging them close. "Welcome to the family, Nita. We are so blessed, the both of us, to have you in our lives."

Ragini Devi couldn't stop the tears from flowing down her face as she looked at her daughter, feeling so proud of her. All the anxiety she had faced while Dayanita was growing up, seemed to be a thing of the past.

Santhini Devi touched her hand to the couple's heads in blessing, before pulling her granddaughter closer to kiss her forehead. "You have made the Thakore name truly proud, my child. This is what true royalty is all about, taking a stand to right a wrong. And you, my dear Harshvardhan, are truly lucky to have my granddaughter as your champion," declared the *Rajmata*.

"I absolutely agree with you, Grandma," he said, hugging the matriarch, his other arm around Dayanita.

Yashwant Mehra waited for the family members to congratulate Harshvardhan and Dayanita on winning the case; as well as for getting engaged, walking forward to shake Harshvardhan's hand vigorously before giving him a hug. "Congrats, bro." He turned to smile at Dayanita. "Hello, Princess Dayanita, I'm Yashwant Mehra, a movie director."

"Hello," said Dayanita, shaking his hand.

"So, you trained in script-writing," he said, tilting his head to look at her. "Can you write me something to match today's courtroom drama?" he asked, grinning.

Dayanita's eyes went wide with wonder. "Do you mean what I think you mean?"

Yashwant nodded. "A grand lady deserves a grand opportunity. I'd love to have a look at whatever you write."

Dayanita squealed in delight, grinning at the director. "That's so awesome. I have one script ready. May I send it over to you?"

"I'd be honoured to play messenger," said her proud *fiancé*, holding her hand tightly in his.

EPILOGUE

Princess Dayanita Thakore and Prince Harshvardhan Singh Gaekwad were married five months later, after Harshvardhan had completed his schedule for *Kuch na Kaho*. In the meanwhile, Yashwant Mehra had been mighty impressed with Dayanita's script and had already approached a producer to back the project with Harshvardhan as the hero.

While Harshvardhan was completing his shoot, she had been busy working with a couple of scriptwriters to translate her plot into Hindi, just the dialogues. Dayanita was excited about the whole thing as she learned a lot during the process.

Kuch na Kaho was set to release six weeks later while Dayanita's film was to go on the floors soon after that. It was the perfect time to tie the knot, they decided and with the blessings of both their families, got married in a simple ceremony at the Thakore palace.

"Are you sure that you don't want the whole pomp and ceremony of a four-day marriage?" Harshvardhan had asked her a month before the wedding.

"What about you?" she asked him in return, raising her face to brush her lips against his rough cheek.

"You know me. I'm not much into socialising. But if you like we can…"

"I don't want to share you with anybody," she declared, nipping his earlobe. "I like to have you all to myself. Okay, maybe I'll let you spend some quality time with Sitara *di*." She grinned mischievously at him.

"Hahaha." Harshvardhan laughed. His sister had become Dayanita's slave. Princess Sitara Devi, who wore her royal status like a shroud, had lightened up a lot since meeting her brother's girlfriend.

"So, are you okay with just a wedding ceremony and reception altogether in one day?" he asked.

"I can't spare one whole day, my prince. Maybe three to four hours?" She fluttered her eyelashes at him.

"You drive a hard bargain, my real princess. But yes, your wish is my royal command," he said, pressing his lips to hers in a deep kiss.

Harshvardhan had a whole month off before beginning promotions for his new release. They decided to go to Bali for their honeymoon where he had hired a villa with an indoor swimming pool in Seminyak for a whole month.

The wedding took place in the morning with five hundred guests gracing the occasion. The married couple left in the early evening to Mumbai to spend their wedding night at their Bandra bungalow.

Dayanita's heart skittered in happiness as she had a long soak in the scented bath, getting ready for their wedding night. Getting out of the bath, she towelled herself dry before applying lotion all over her body. She then pulled on the transparent negligee in virginal white, giving her reflection in the mirror a wicked grin.

Stepping out of the bathroom, she ran her eyes around the bedroom, looking for her husband of a few hours. "Harsh?"

"Here you go," he said, pushing a trolley ahead of him as he entered the bedroom, wearing a pair of shorts and nothing else.

Dayanita's eyes went wide when she noticed the bottle of champagne buried in a bucket of ice, the two red roses tucked into a blue-glazed ceramic vase and a bowl of strawberries with cream. "I like your style," she declared, walking up to her husband and hugging him, rubbing her face on his naked chest like a small kitten, mewling in pleasure.

"Wait a minute, let me look at you," he said, pushing her away from him even as he held her hands. He whistled, his grey eyes turning smoky with desire as he eyed her sexy body through the thin veil of the gown as it followed her curves faithfully to fall below her knees. "You look beautiful," he said, pulling her into his arms to kiss her.

"And you look fabulous," she said, her voice breathless as she looked up into his handsome face. "I can't believe we are married," she said, going on tiptoe to bite his lower lip.

He groaned, lifting his hands to hold her head steady as he kissed her again. "I love you, babe, from the bottom of my heart."

"And I love you, my prince. You are the best thing that has ever happened to me." She pushed him on the bed to climb over him, kissing him enthusiastically, her lips trailing all over his face before zeroing in on his mouth.

He turned her over to lie on top of her, pinning her arms at her side. "I want to be inside you, now."

"Hmm… I have a condition though."

"Tell me woman, before I die of frustration," he groaned, bending down to bite her nipple over her negligee.

"Harsh…" Dayanita moaned in turn, dragging his head closer to her body, "I need you so."

"And what's your damn condition? You haven't told me yet," he said, lifting his head to blow on the damp nipple, making it tighten, laughing even as he refused to oblige her when she would have pulled his head down to her breast again.

"I don't want you to use a condom," she said, lifting her face to bite his shoulder. "Harsh, my body's screaming for you. Are you going to do something about it?" she demanded.

He rolled off her before lifting her up and pulling off her negligee before clamping his lips to her breast, suckling on it deeply even as he held the second breast with his hand while his other hand travelled south to caress her femininity, using his fingers cleverly, making her buck in his arms.

"Oh yes, Harsh! Yes," she moaned long and loud, thrashing her legs as her body trembled with a powerful orgasm that shook her to the very core.

It was a while before she got her breath back. She reached out to touch his tumescent shaft, guiding him into her vagina, wrapping her legs around his waist, her body rejoicing as he pounded into her, his lips at her throat as he dragged his tongue over her pulse points, before he groaned long and hard, pouring his seed into her for the first time since they began making love.

"Nita, babe, that was simply amazing," he swore, flopping down on her.

She refused to let him go when he would have moved, not wanting to crush her with his weight. "No, Harsh, I need you on me," she said, revelling in his warmth as she hugged him close, her hands caressing his back.

She got up after a while to open the champagne bottle and pour some into two glasses, carrying them over to the bed.

Harshvardhan lay back on the bed, his hands steeped under his head as he eyed his new wife in all her naked glory. "Come here," he said.

"Is that an order, your royal highness?" she asked, her voice shaking with laughter as she placed the champagne glasses on a side table in a hurry when he tumbled her in his arms. Her eyes went wide when she felt his hardening shaft against her belly. "My, my, aren't we in a hurry? Isn't that too quick a recovery?" she teased, bending down to rub her face on his hair roughened chest, enjoying the friction.

"That's what you do to me, my real princess," he said, gathering her close for an encore.

THE END

REFERENCES

1. Indian Royalty: https://www.scoopwhoop.com

2. Studying in Los Angeles: https://study.com/articles/Los_Angeles_California_City_and_Higher_Education_Facts.html

3. Los Angeles Film School: http://campaign.columbiacollege.edu/screenwriting-degree

4. Script writing courses in Mumbai: http://www.mdfa.co.in/script-writing-courses.html

5. The Beverly Hills Hotel: https://www.dorchestercollection.com/en/los-angeles/the-beverly-hills-hotel/rooms-suites/garden-suite/

6. Talent agency Mumbai: http://www.bollywoodcareer.com/4-best-casting-agencies-in-mumbai/

7. #metoo: https://www.news18.com/news/immersive/indias-metoo-woman.html

8. Disneyland: https://disneyland.disney.go.com/

OTHER BOOKS
BY
SUNDARI VENKATRAMAN

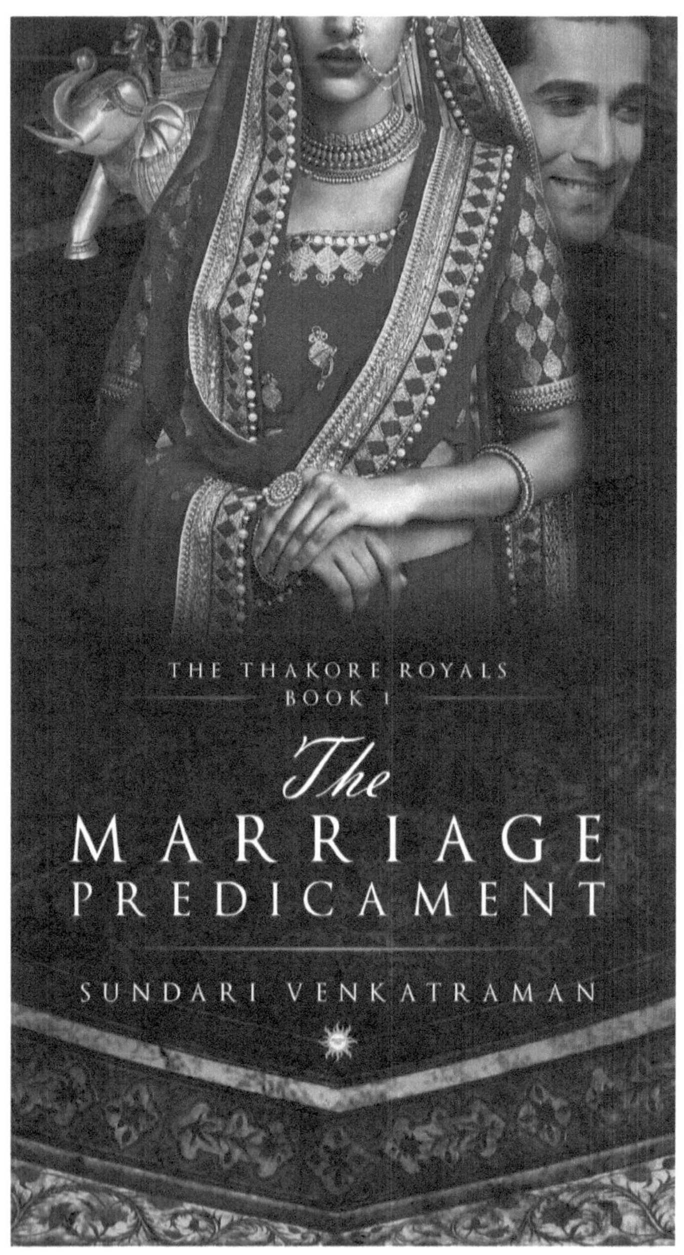
THE THAKORE ROYALS
BOOK 1
The
MARRIAGE
PREDICAMENT
SUNDARI VENKATRAMAN

Princess Yashodhara Jadeja of Bhatewar isn't at all keen to get married. With her tarnished past, she knows that her married life would never be easy. But, between her father's Will and her mother's persuasion, she's left with no choice.

Prince Indrajeet Thakore of Udaipur agrees to meet Yashodhara as a prospective wife after his grandmother, Rajmata Santhini Devi, persuades him. While no cymbals crash at their first meeting, the couple grow to like and respect one another before they agree to tie the knot.

Both belong to royal families and both have responsibilities. Over and above all that, their marriage is plagued by a predicament, just as Yashodhara had expected. It looks like they can lead a happy married life only if the princess is willing to break a promise. Will she be able to do that? And will Prince Indrajeet continue to love her once he gets to know about her past?

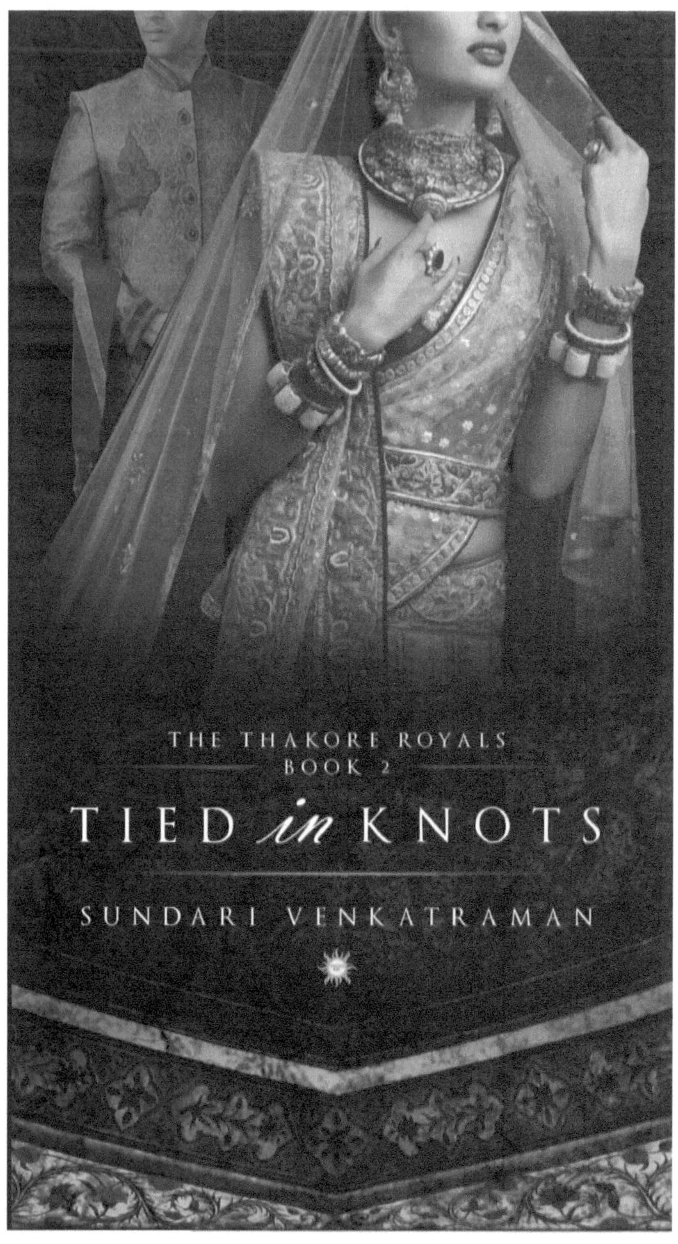

THE THAKORE ROYALS
BOOK 2
TIED in KNOTS
SUNDARI VENKATRAMAN

When Princess Chitrangada Vasudeva of Jodhana runs away from her bodyguards in the European city of Zurich, the last thing she expects is to be incarcerated with a stranger in his hotel suite for three days and nights.

Prince Rajvardhan Thakore of Udaipur is on his way to take part in the ice polo event at St. Moritz and plans to take a much-needed break in Zurich. He's thrown for a toss when he stops his car to help a damsel in distress. A few minutes into the encounter, he finds out that "Princess" is anything but a helpless female.

Sparks fly, and how!

Until that morning when Princess simply ups and leaves Rajvardhan without a contact number or a forwarding address. He doesn't even know her real name.

And then they meet again under the most unusual of circumstances back in Rajasthan, during Chitrangada's engagement to Raja Harischandra Gajanan of Indore. Even stranger is the fact that her fiancé is more her father's contemporary than hers.

Will the Thakore prince's endeavor to make the Vasudeva princess his own succeed under the circumstances?

Man Friday
SUNDARI VENKATRAMAN

ituraj realises he's in love with the Gaekwad princess, Sitara Devi. The timing is slightly wrong though. Just ten minutes ago Sitara Devi married Harishchandra Gajanan. All of seventeen and nursing a badly bruised heart, Rituraj takes up boxing, hoping to build his strength and heal his wounded soul.

When destiny gives them a second chance, hope springs in his heart.

Rituraj grabs the opportunity of becoming Sitara's bodyguard-cum-assistant. He's the only man in her life but he's just her Man Friday. Since his father was merely an employee of Sitara's father, will he even be considered as a prospective life partner for the Gaekwad princess?

Sitara and Rituraj are crazily attracted to each other, yet they are unable to move forward. So where is the hitch? Why the fear in taking the relationship to the next level?

Class Barriers! Debauchery! Sexual Perversion!

It looks like 'Ne'er the twain shall meet'.

Read the book to find out if Sitara eventually gets together with her Man Friday.

Connect with Sundari Venkatraman here:

Sundari Venkatraman Books

Sundari Venkatraman Books

https://www.sundarivenkatraman.in

Author Sundari Venkatraman

@sundarivenkat

@sundarivenkatraman

sundarivenkat@gmail.com

For Colin and Margaret,
Pam, and Ozzie